Mu
Act

By Hugh Morrison

MONTPELIER PUBLISHING
2023

© Hugh Morrison 2023

All rights reserved. No part of this publication may be reproduced, stored in a retrieval system, or transmitted, in any form or by any means without the prior written permission of the publisher, nor be otherwise circulated in any form of binding or cover other than that in which it is published and without a similar condition including this condition being imposed on the subsequent purchaser.

Published in Great Britain by Montpelier Publishing.
Set in Palatino Linotype 10.5 point
Cover image by Miguna Studio
ISBN: 9798390128992

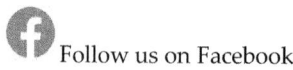 Follow us on Facebook

Chapter One

'It's another of those letters,' said an angry voice from behind the wall.

The Reverend Lucian Shaw, vicar of All Saint's Church in the Suffolk village of Lower Addenham, was on the other side of the wall, and at first thought the statement was intended for him. Then he heard a woman's voice in reply, and realised that his presence was undetected. He saw the postman cycling away up the hill; a letter had presumably arrived in the morning post.

'Oh Bert, not again,' the woman said plaintively.

Shaw paused in his walk; the high wall divided the back yard of the little village general stores from the high street; he had only left the vicarage to buy some pipe tobacco but he now realised he had inadvertently become an eavesdropper.

He resolved to ignore the conversation. But the man spoke again, more angrily this time.

'Always sends them by post, never by hand, and never signs 'em. But it's from her, all right. I recognise the handwriting from those notices she's always putting up in the village hall. And look at this part.'

There was a moment of silence and then the woman spoke again.

'Oh Bert, she wouldn't. How did she know that?'

'I've no idea,' replied the man. 'But we could lose the

post office if that comes out. I'm going to have it out with her right this minute.'

Shaw sighed. He did not listen to village gossip, but had heard rumours through his wife that Mrs Cranston, the young shop-keeper, had been subjected to some rather unpleasant poison-pen letters. That, Shaw decided, went beyond the realms of gossip and was something that ought to be stamped out. He decided to compromise by walking at a slightly slower pace than usual alongside the brick wall, and if he should hear anything, well, then that would be unavoidable.

He did not have to wait long. Audrey Cranston spoke again. 'Please don't make a fuss Bert. Just let it be.'

'No I won't,' said Cranston gruffly. 'I'll calm down a little first, I'll grant you that, – but I'm having it out with her. You mark my words. And if she don't stop this nonsense, so help me, I'll…'

Cranston's intention remained unspoken as a little bell rang from within the shop. Shaw by this time could legitimately dawdle no longer, and had reached the shop door and pushed it open.

Later, as Shaw sat down to luncheon in the little Georgian vicarage, he felt that all was right with the world. After a murky start it had turned into one of those bright, still February days on which, if one sat in the chair by the window in the sunlight, one might almost think it were summer. As an economical gesture his wife, Marion, had even instructed Hettie, the maid of all work, not to bother lighting the fire in the dining room. It felt almost as if spring was on its way.

That, thought Shaw, was a warning sign. When he had such feelings of contentment – bordering on complacency – it invariably meant that Something Was About to Happen. A tall, slim man in middle age, with a full head of iron-grey hair, Shaw undertook the slight contortions required to fit into the replica Jacobean carver chair at the head of the table in the small dining room. His wife, Marion, a few years younger than him and still with something of the fading bloom of youth about her, sat opposite; Fraser, their little West Highland terrier sat at his mistress' feet, hoping for some morsel of food, despite sensing the disapproval of his master of the habit of feeding animals from the table.

'*Benedictus benedicat, per Jesum Christum Dominum Nostrum, Amen.*' Shaw pronounced his old Cambridge college Grace, something he took pride in saying meaningfully at every single meal.

He lifted the lid of the salver.

'Ah. Boiled mutton again, I see,' he said.

'I'm sorry sir,' blurted Hettie, who stood close by, 'but there was rather a lot left over from...'

'That is quite all right, Hettie,' said Shaw. 'We must all spend a little less in these troubled times. And you are so good at dressing things up in different ways.'

Hettie blushed. 'Shall I serve, sir?'

'That's all right, we'll manage ourselves,' said Shaw. 'Off you go.'

'Very good sir,' said Hettie with a quick bob, and then withdrew.

'You're not normally as dismissive,' said Mrs Shaw. 'Am I to assume there is something you wish to discuss *pas devant les domestiques*?'

'La *domestique*, my dear,' corrected Shaw with a wry smile. 'We only have one servant.'

'Quite,' replied his wife. 'Come along now, I know when you've got something on your mind.'

'It may be nothing,' said Shaw, 'but I couldn't help overhearing something in the village this morning.'

'Oh dear. That is generally the precursor to something rather unpleasant, I fear. What part of the village, may I ask?'

'The general stores.'

Mrs Shaw sighed and looked down as she struggled to slice through a piece of mutton. 'Connected, I suspect, with some nasty letters?'

'It would seem so. May I know a little more?'

'I did mention it before but you told me you were not interested in village gossip.'

'I fear it may be about to go beyond that.'

'Very well. It seems poor young Audrey Cranston, as if she hadn't enough to put up with, has received two or three anonymous letters in the post. Nothing threatening, or anything like that ought to be shown to the police, but just, well, nasty. Alluding to things about her.'

'Th...er, things?' asked Shaw, clearing his throat after swallowing a particularly tough piece of mutton.

'You know. It was bad enough her losing her baby when it was just a month old, but then to be told after that by the doctors that she couldn't have any more...'

'Of course, I remember,' said Shaw sadly. 'The funeral of an infant tends to stick in the memory. But I was not aware of the other piece of news. How dreadful.'

'It's common knowledge in the village,' said Mrs Shaw, 'so it could be anybody sending those letters. But really, who would be so beastly as to mock someone for that?'

'Mr Cranston said that he knew who it was from, and that he was going to confront the writer.'

'How dramatic!' replied Mrs Shaw. 'Did he tell you who

the writer was?'

'Ah...no,' replied Shaw. 'We did not speak.'

'Then how did you...?'

Shaw sighed. 'I was eavesdropping, I confess.'

'That's almost inevitable in a little village like this. Do go on.'

'Mr Cranston said he would "have it out" with the writer.'

'Of course one doesn't like to name names...' mused Mrs Shaw, as she gave up on the last gristly portion of meat on her plate. 'But I think it must be something to do with LADS.'

'Lads?' asked Shaw. 'But Mr Cranston distinctly said he would have it out with "her".'

'I don't mean lads as in boys, Lucian,' said Mrs Shaw. 'I mean L-A-D-S. It's a...what do they call it...an acronym.'

These acronyms, thought Shaw, seemed to have proliferated since the war, and he wished they had not done so. He pondered for a moment until he realised what it stood for.

'The Lower Addenham Dramatic Society, you mean?' he said.

'That's right,' replied Mrs Shaw brightly. 'They're putting on *Hamlet* this evening and Mrs Cranston is playing Ophelia. I know because I offered to help Madame with the costumes.'

'Madame?' asked Shaw.

'Yes, you know. The Belgian woman who runs that little boutique where the Cokeleys used to have their antique shop.'

'Ah, yes,' said Shaw. 'I don't believe I know her.'

'You wouldn't,' said Mrs Shaw. 'She's Catholic of course so doesn't come to our church, and I'd hardly expect you to be visiting a gown shop.'

'Indeed.'

'Anyway, I was having a look inside and we got chatting and it turns out she's not only involved in costume for the play but is playing Hamlet's mother as well. So it's rather a lot of work for her and I offered to help on the show nights.'

'Most kind of you,' replied her husband. 'We ought to support these events.'

'It's the technical rehearsal then the opening night tonight,' replied Mrs Shaw. 'I'd almost forgotten I promised to attend. I suspect it's somebody there that Mr Cranston intends to confront.'

'Go on,' said Shaw cautiously.

'Madame was telling me they've been having trouble with one of the members. A Mrs Hexham.'

'Trouble...?'

'She's, well, difficult.'

'Ah. I don't believe I know her, either.'

'She was apparently something of a pillar of the Baptists. If one can have pillars of a tin chapel, that is. Perhaps they have girders? At any rate, she had some sort of falling-out with the minister and swore she'd never set foot in a church again.'

'She has something of a history of being difficult, perhaps?' asked Shaw.

'Yes,' replied his wife. 'Madame wasn't sure if she was just some sort of English eccentric and so she spoke to me about it to make certain. She – Mrs Hexham, that is, had a terrifically embarrassing outburst of temper during a rehearsal, frightening some of the children and causing several of the new members to walk out. It wasn't the first time either. The committee, which Madame is on, tried to discuss it in a meeting but she refused to turn up, so they felt they had no option but to give notice to withdraw her membership once the current production is finished.'

'I see,' said Shaw. 'But the committee still has sufficient need of her not to dismiss her immediately.'

'She and her husband do work awfully hard for the society and to be honest,' replied his wife, 'the whole thing is likely to fall to bits if they go. That's why the committee gave her notice that they intended to vote her out after the production.'

'Oh dear,' said Shaw. 'Dramatic passions. I am glad we have nothing of the kind in the church. This Mrs...Hexham is, presumably, suspected of sending the letters to Mrs Cranston?'

'Not much doubt about it,' said Mrs Shaw. 'Why would anyone else bother?'

'A grudge-bearer, perhaps...' mused Shaw. 'But from what Mr Cranston said it seemed the most recent letter to his wife had gone much further. He sounded angry enough to be capable of anything. I feel I ought to intervene in some way, but then again, it really is none of my business.'

'Look here,' said his wife. 'Why don't you come along to the dress rehearsal tonight? They're looking for a prompt – old Mr Hawtrey has had to cancel again due to his chest. I'll run along and tell the director you'd like to help and that will give you the perfect excuse to be there if anything happens.'

'Ought not the director take the lead in settling this matter with Mrs Hexham?' asked Shaw. 'What is his name?'

'Oh dear, no,' said Mrs Shaw shaking her head. 'It's a she, not a he. Old Mrs Bardell – the director, I mean – is in rather a world of her own. Artistic, you know, and rather lives in the past. She was a professional actress years ago – on the London stage – and is awfully good at encouraging everybody and bearing them up, but I'm afraid dealing with any problems off-stage is completely beyond her.'

Joan Hexham sat in her study like a spider at the centre of a web of village gossip and intrigue. She, of course, did not not think of herself in such arachnoid terms, but pictured herself more as a chess player, presiding over a board of pieces representing various people in her life that she had an interest in controlling.

Any movement of an individual piece had to be considered relative to the others, and she was always thinking several moves ahead. The ultimate goal, of course, was for the protection of her king, which represented her own interests.

She sat back in her chair with a contented sigh, sealing the last of her letters, to be delivered discretely to the pillar box under cover of darkness.

A rotund woman of an uncertain age with alarmingly bright flame-red hair, (a product of the dyer's art rather than nature), Mrs Hexham was known by, and avoided by, most people in the village. She had not been born in the village but, when she had still a certain charm of youth about her, had married a successful local seed merchant before the war, giving herself a step up the social ladder in the process.

From a long line of Baptist farmers, she had all of the faults of her Puritan forebears with none of their redeeming Christian virtues. An overbearing manner and waspish, vengeful attitude towards any perceived slight, soon alienated her from village life and she had walked out of, or been quietly expelled from, every institution from the Baptist chapel to the Women's Institute.

She had gradually moved down the social scale in this regard; initial attempts to curry favour with the gentry by volunteering for wartime nursing duties at the local manor had been met with flat refusal ('that *ghastly* woman' Lady Addenham had called her, deliberately within earshot).

The middle classes, she found, were easier for her to manipulate as their politeness made them less likely to snub her so readily. She had eventually come to rest in what was her perfect milieux; the Lower Addenham Dramatic Society, which met in the village hall.

She had no particular love of the theatre nor culture in general, but she required an outlet for her manipulative energies, or what she would call her organisational skills. The great advantage of the LADS (as the organisation was known) was a chronic shortage of administrators. There was no lack of star-struck youngsters wanting to 'strut and fret upon the stage' as Shakespeare put it, but most of them were hopeless at anything else such as organising the properties or the scenery.

Her husband Reginald was the perfect companion in this endeavour; a skilled general handyman, he was able to turn his hand to pretty much anything from lighting to scenery painting to properties manufacture. Between them, over the years, they had made themselves indispensable; Mrs Hexham had become the permanently unopposed Madam President, and as her sense of indispensability grew, so in turn had shrunk her inhibitions and what little remained of her good grace.

Not helped by the 'change of life,' and fading looks, her moods had worsened. This had culminated recently in her throwing a hideous and highly embarrassing tantrum in the village hall, accusing the entire company of uselessness and laziness, which resulted in some of the younger female members walking out in tears and vowing never to return.

What was remarkable was that nobody seemed to stand up to her. In previous organisations she had belonged to, somebody had always eventually confronted her and got rid of her ('trying to stand in her way,' she called it). The members of the LADS, however, who opposed her had simply drifted away and she was left now as the *de facto* and unchallengeable leader of the group.

Mrs Hexham frowned and patted her scarlet hair in place as she closed the lid of her bureau. Now, she reflected, there had been A Challenge, and this could not be allowed to stand.

Her thoughts were interrupted by an apologetic knock at the door.

'Yes,' said Mrs Hexham. She assumed it would be Mrs Burridge, her daily. Live-in servants she had none, as none could put up with her for long, but she had found her equal in Mrs Burridge, who held a similar position to her as head gossip in the neighbouring village of Addenham Magna. The pair sometimes even helped each other by divulging useful pieces of local intelligence.

It was not, however, Mrs Burridge who appeared at the door, but her own husband, Reginald. A slim, slightly built man with rugged, almost handsome features, he stood only an inch or so taller than his wife and had a quiet, almost apologetic air about him.

'Just off to the shop in Netley,' he said vaguely, as he shrugged on his overcoat and took his bowler hat from the hall-stand by the study door. He owned three shops and a wholesale seed store, which more or less ran themselves, but he took it upon himself to visit them in turn every so often 'to keep the staff on their toes' as he called it.

'Keep an eye on that one with the squint,' said his wife.

'He'll have his fingers in the till if you don't.'

'Leonards?' asked Mr Hexham uninterestedly. 'He wouldn't dare. You leave him to me.'

Mrs Hexham murmured reluctant assent. In matters of her husband's business, she had learned to keep her distance years ago. After a particularly persistent interrogation of him about the shops, her normally acquiescent spouse had dumped a stack of ledgers on her desk and said vehemently 'If you think you can run this business better than I can, you're welcome to it – if you can sort that lot out!'

This had frightened her somewhat, as she knew she was out of her depth. Responsibility for her own actions scared her, for what she craved more than anything was the highly alluring and addictive combination of power without responsibility.

This did not stop her, however, from discretely prying into her husband's business correspondence from time to time by means of a steaming kettle; a recent police case over financial irregularity in at least one of the shops had perturbed her, especially since the culprit had never been identified. She had been dropping hints on this topic for some time, but her husband did not seem to notice.

'I'm off then,' said Mr Hexham, kissing his wife perfunctorily on her heavily powdered left jowl. 'All set for tonight's show?'

Mrs Hexham smiled. 'Oh yes. I think I've got everyone just where I want them. Once this production's over there won't be any more nonsense about getting rid of me.'

'Good-oh,' said Mr Hexham. 'Disgraceful the way they think they can just get rid of you – of both of us, like that.'

'I think they'll reconsider quite soon,' said Mrs Hexham, as she continued to smile. 'I've got them all where I want them, you see.'

'All who?'

'The conspirators. The ones who think they are going to vote me out. But I've learned some interesting things about them that will make them reconsider that.'

'What sort of things?'

'Never you mind. But it's surprising what you can find out for a few shillings paid to a newspaper cuttings agency just by giving them a name. And servants will talk for even less, if you know the right servants. There was one I didn't even have to pay a penny for, that silly Gladys Kersey.'

'Barmaid at the George?' enquired Mr Hexham cautiously. Officially, he did not take strong drink – a nod to his non-conformist background – but Mrs Hexham knew he occasionally indulged at the village pubs. She permitted him to attend, on the tacit understanding that he would report anything interesting that he heard, as such places were rife with gossip.

'What do you want with her?' he continued. 'She's not on the committee.'

'No, but she told me some very useful information about someone who *is*,' said his wife. 'The stupid girl seems to think I'm some sort of friendly aunt and practically begged me to let myself into her confidence.'

'Useful,' said Mr Hexham blandly. 'Lucky you were able to get the gen on all the voting members.'

'It wasn't luck, my dear,' replied his wife. 'I made sure everyone I persuaded to join the committee, were those as I already had some "gen" on. I knew it might come in useful for times like these.'

A reluctant smile spread briefly across Mr Hexham's face. 'Very clever. Ta-ta then'.

As her husband shut the front door behind him, Mrs Hexham straightened the papers on her desk and begun humming an air from last year's production of *The Mikado*.

Clarence Weekes caught sight of himself in the mirror above the seats as he sat down in the railway compartment on the train to work. He breathed a sigh of relief as nobody else got on and the train departed, meaning he would have some time to himself before the little branch-line train from Lower Addenham arrived in Great Netley.

Knowing he was alone, he stood up and looked at himself in the mirror again, adjusting his tie and pocket handkerchief and tucking back a wisp of black hair under the brim of his hat, noticing the roots had begun to go grey again. He rubbed his jowls; age seemed to have caught up with him for good this time. He made a mental note to buy some more of a certain hair preparation from the chemist's, and sat back down.

He opened the letter that had arrived in the post at his cottage that morning.

> Well, Polonius, or as it says in the play, 'tedious old fool.' It seems you have decided to become strong and manly for once in your life and get rid of a woman you do not like. It does not surprise me, dear, as I suspect you are not the sort that likes too many women around him, except perhaps your mother. Before you cast your vote just remember one thing. There are those of us who know a little bit about you. Such things as newspaper libraries have all sorts of interesting things in them. I dare say your employer and your landlord would not be happy if they knew. I do not think the vicar would want you in his choir either, and mother definitely would not approve…

Weekes' hands trembled as he placed the letter back in his pocket. It was not signed but he was in no doubt as to who had sent it. The bitch, the *bloody* bitch, he thought to himself.

This was blackmail, pure and simple. And blackmail over something so bloody silly as a blasted amateur dramatics group. She didn't even want money! He wished he had never got involved in the first place. But it was so lonely out in the village and he had never found it easy to make friends.

The church choir, and the amateur theatricals, had enabled him to shine in a way he never could in his accountancy job in Midchester. What was more, it was a way of keeping him away from…other places. He had tried and tried, even seen doctors about it after the trial, but nothing had worked.

One quack, calling him a hopeless case, had even recommended he move abroad somewhere more tolerant, such as the near east, but that would mean leaving his mother, all alone in her genteel Eastbourne hotel; he saw her little enough now as it was.

Instead, he had decided to move out of London to some remote country spot where he was unknown and there would be less temptation. His employer, whom he suspected shared his affliction, instead of outright dismissal had discretely arranged for a transfer to a rural branch of the firm. Until now, it seemed to have gone well.

At first, 'that woman' had been friendly to him and he had been quite impressed by her indomitable nature. Strong women had always appealed to him. But now…well, there was nothing for it. As the train slowed down with a sound of rattling metal over the points at Great Netley, he made a decision: either he would have to go, or she would.

Ronald Havering, Ronnie to his friends and many acquaintances, rolled over in bed and looked at the alarm clock. Past nine, he realised he had missed breakfast and would now have nothing but congealed scrambled eggs left under a plate on the sideboard. Curse all blasted servants, he thought to himself, and their blasted punctuality, as if they owned the house instead of him.

It was not his house though, he remembered sullenly, but that of his parents. At 25, they were regularly dropping hints that he ought to be married, with a proper job and with a place of his own instead of living off them and, in their words, 'playing at being a writer.'

His bedroom in the eaves of the large, rambling Tudor house on the edge of Lower Addenham was cold and draughty (his father considered fires in bedrooms a decadent luxury) and he struggled to put his dressing gown on under the covers. He stood up, shuffling his feet into his slippers, and felt his head and stomach lurch simultaneously; it had been quite a night in the George.

He saw two half crowns and some coppers on the bedside table and realised that was probably all he had left of the monthly allowance his parents gave him. There was a crumpled packet of De Reske cigarettes with two left inside, and he sullenly lit one. He opened his dressing gown and urinated loudly into the chamber pot beside the bed, already half full from the results of last night's drinking.

Christ, he thought, my head hurts. He lay back on the bed and thought about what he would do today. Write, he supposed. He had been working for almost two years on a blank verse play entitled *Workers' Paradise*, set in the England of 1940, in which socialism and free love had triumphed and a young, handsome leader (not dissimilar to himself) had ousted the government to rule absolutely over a workers' soviet.

He had already had some interest shown by an impresario friend of someone he had known at Oxford, some 'awful pansy' who went by the name of Adrian de la Touche, if you please, (his real name was Abraham Gluckstein) and now all he needed to do was finish the bally thing and that would be him made.

He caught sight of himself in the mirror on his chest of drawers. His dark good looks astonished him sometimes, even now when he was unshaven with his hair dishevelled. Closing one eye against the wisps of smoke rising from his cigarette, he combed his hair and posed in front of the mirror. Yes, he thought. Work on the play, then a few drinks at the George afterwards. Without thinking, he recited the lines from Hamlet.

'"O that this too, too solid flesh should melt…"'

Blast it, tonight was the night of that bloody silly play at the village hall, he remembered. He had only signed up for it because he had been trying to impress that Gladys. She had heard he was 'something to do with the theatre,' and would be 'just right for Hamlet' and with a strict father like hers, it was the only way he could see her regularly without all that working-class courting nonsense where a girl was supposed to immediately marry anyone she was seen 'going steady' with.

Silly little star-struck Gladys the barmaid, with her yokel voice but face and figure fit for the pages of *La Vie Parisienne*, and what was more, she barely knew it, unlike some little tarts he knew who thought they were God's gift to men. The thought of her made him feel revulsion and lust at the same time. He wondered if he had any chance of getting that started up again, and decided no, it would be impossible now, after what had happened.

Besides, the girl would barely speak to him now and only refrained from cutting him stone dead at rehearsals because she was afraid others might notice. That French woman, or was she Belgian, playing Hamlet's mother – now she was looking *decidedly* promising. Older than him, of course, but that usually meant they had a bit of experience and would be less likely to just lie there like a sack of potatoes. He grinned and smoothed his hair back. There was a knock at the door.

'If that's breakfast in bed Maeve, I'll love you forever.'

He pulled the door open to find the Irish maid-of-all work standing in the oak-beamed corridor. She gave him a disdainful look.

'Forever's about three weeks with you, from what I've heard,' she said with a look of disgust.

Havering laughed loudly. Maeve wasn't a bad sort, he thought to himself. Good figure and not a bad face, but she was one of those fiery redheads with a temper, who would probably stab you in the night if you got on the wrong side of her.

His parents thought her over-familiar, but, the servant shortage being what is was, they had to put up with her. Not worth making a move on, he thought, but at least something to look at when she was bending over to light the fire, and didn't she know it.

'If oi convert to de true faith will yez have me den, Maeve me love?' he asked in a broad Irish brogue.

'God would strike you down the moment you stepped in a Catholic church, so He would,' said Maeve. 'And it's not breakfast I'm bringing you, it's a letter.'

'A letther is it you're afther bringing himself?' exclaimed Havering, continuing his stage-Irish act. 'Sure I didn't hear the knock o' the postman; has the puir old front door himself been blown up by the freedom fighters of the Republic?'

'Don't be making jokes about things like that,' said Maeve briskly, her face now assuming the mask of a professional servant.

'Sure, we Irish are a peace-loving race,' continued Havering in his brogue, 'and by God I'll fight any man that says otherwise.'

'That's enough fooling,' chided Maeve, but Havering could see she was suppressing a smile. 'It must have come by the early post, I only just saw it on the mat.'

She handed him the letter. 'If that'll be all, sir?'

Before Havering had had time to reply, Maeve had bustled off down the corridor.

Havering shrugged and went back into his bedroom. He jumped on the bed, lit the last cigarette in the packet, and opened the letter.

Expecting some sort of *billet doux* – perhaps from Gladys wanting to revive their affair – his eyes widened as he took in the text of the letter.

Dear Hamlet, or should I say, Casanova,

You have been a naughty boy, haven't you? 'To be or not to be' is your famous line. Well someone is never going to be anything now because of what you did. I know what you arranged for your little strumpet, the silly girl told me all about it because she needed a shoulder to cry on and God knows she was not going to get that from you. She told me she didn't have anyone else to talk to and could I keep a secret? Well yes I can, Hamlet dear, but only if you make sure a certain person does not get voted off the committee. I wonder what Gladys' father would think. I wonder what the police will think of it?

This time, Havering could not resist the wave of nausea that overcame him, and vomited in the already full chamberpot. He read the letter again. It was unsigned, but he had no doubt who it was from. A cold sensation of hatred flooded his body. He laughed bitterly at the absurdity of it; being blackmailed by some puritanical nobody from a gimcrack village-hall theatrical troupe.

He had half a mind to just go along with it; he was not going to take part in any more plays so could not care less who ran the blasted thing. But then...she would always have that incriminating evidence on him. He had read that blackmailers always came back if you gave in to them. Next time she might want money. He cursed Gladys; why on earth did she have to confide in that ridiculous Hexham woman?

Then he remembered Gladys' mother was dead; she probably had nobody else to talk to, and must have had some silly working-class guilt about what had happened; God knew it had been difficult enough to get her to agree to it.

He snorted; difficult for *her*! It had cost *him* ten guineas, plus her train fare to London, and had to be arranged clandestinely by a chap who knew a chap who knew a chap, all of whom wanted a cut for themselves.

He felt a twinge of conscience, but quickly pushed it out of his mind. If the police were involved...that would mean being cut off from his parents' money for sure, and if the papers got hold of it, it could seriously damage his reputation as a playwright.

He realised he had to make sure that Joan Hexham would keep her ugly lipstick-coated mouth shut permanently.

Chapter Two

Mrs Charles Haskins, or Madame Helene Dubois, as she was better known in Lower Addenham, looked down at the letter she was holding, her hands quivering with anger. She wondered what she had done to deserve being insulted in such a way.

She was in the ladies' boutique she ran in the High Street. She had got the place cheap because of some *crime passionel** that had occurred in the place when it had been an antiques shop; apparently the English were squeamish about living somewhere where violent death had occurred.

She laughed bitterly at the thought. Belgians such as herself could afford no such sentimentality; every street of her home town had witnessed violent death during the occupation of *les Boches.* Life had to go on. She felt a twinge of homesickness for Belgium, and her thoughts drifted back to the past.

She had come from a poor family but with a pretty face, a quick wit and a head for figures she had soon begun to be an asset to her father's little bistro in the outskirts of Liège. Then, just after her eighteenth birthday, the Germans had invaded and the Rape of Belgium had begun. She swallowed back tears as she looked down at the letter.

*See A Third Class Murder

How had this...this....*vielle vache* who had written it known what had happened? And how could she use it as blackmail, to keep her place on her stupid theatrical group? She had been forced into what had happened in the war; had been offered the choice only of compliance, or death.

Madame Dubois took a deep breath and gritted her teeth. She felt cold fury flood her body. It was ridiculous, to allow this dried-up English *chienne* to make her cry. She had not cried properly, she realised, since...since the events alluded to in the letter.

She had been one of the lucky ones, packed off under the auspices of the Red Cross to England in 1915, as part of the first wave of Belgian refugees, when the English were still war-happy and welcoming. She was too old, really, and ought to have stayed in Liege, but her family had insisted; who knew what further horrors the Hun would inflict on the nation's womanhood.

She was given a job as a maid to Charles Haskins, a wealthy bachelor of independent means twenty-five years her senior, who had soon fallen for her coquettish charms and married her, much to the anger of the other servants. Her son Henry or Henri, as she called him, had been born a year later.

Then her husband had been killed. Too old and unfit for military service at first, he had kept on trying and by 1917 as the army became desperate for human fuel to feed the ravenous inferno of the war, he finally got a commission in the Army Pay Department, and was promptly killed by a shell the day after he arrived in France.

She was heartbroken, but there was more heartache to come. The war ended and she learned her parents had been killed and their café destroyed in the Allied offensive of 1918. There was no home to go back to.

She lived on in relative luxury in the Suffolk manor

house she had come to as a servant. Running a bar was one thing, but understanding her late husband's complex investments was another, and when the 'crash' of 1929 came, she was virtually penniless. She was able to fund a small annuity and to keep Henry in his boarding school by selling the house.

She then sank the last of her money into setting up a small second-hand boutique in an empty shop in Lower Addenham. The initial stock comprised mainly of her huge collection of expensive clothes and accessories she now no longer had room for in the little cottage she rented on the edge of the village; a house smaller even than the one she had lived in as a girl in Liège.

She had been surprised at the success of the shop, especially amongst the younger village girls who shared her slim figure, and she soon began visiting other second hand clothes shops, jumble sales, estate sales and so on to pick out good quality pieces which she then cleaned, repaired and sold on for a profit.

The English country folk, she realised, lived rather drab lives, especially the working people, and she had somehow been able to give a little continental glamour to the village women at an affordable price. The local people assumed, naturally enough, she was French, and so the little shop was decorated with pictures of Paris, the Riviera and so on. Of course, she could not call the place Haskins', so used her maiden name with Madame instead of *Mademoiselle*.

Before long she was well-known in the village and cautiously welcomed (for the English, being an island race, were wary of foreigners). She had agreed to help with the costumes for the dramatic society's production of *Hamlet*, in exchange for free advertising in the programme, but then, to her amazement, had been asked to take on the part of Hamlet's mother by the director, Joan Hexham, who then also invited her to be a part of the group's committee.

Somewhat lonely, she gladly accepted, soon acquiring a male admirer also, although there was, she reflected, something of an age difference between them. Although she struggled slightly with the antiquated English of Shakespeare, she was a natural performer and had been looking forward to the show, at least until recently.

She had noticed that Joan Hexham was an odd character; her oddities had been concealed at first by her Englishness, and Madame Dubois had assumed she was just another English eccentric who needed to be humoured. But then after guarded conversations with the other members of the group she realised the woman was a menace and perhaps even unbalanced.

She had even mentioned it to Mrs Shaw, the wife of *le prêtre* – she still found it odd to think of priests having wives – who had agreed with her that Mrs Hexham was, as she politely put it, 'difficult'.

It was too late now to back out of the show, but she had agreed with the others that Mrs Hexham should be quietly 'retired' from the group. It seemed, however, that Mrs Hexham did not wish to go quietly. Madame Dubois looked at the letter again and her fists curled in anger around the paper as she pictured Mrs Hexham writing on it. I have lost my husband and my family and my country, she thought to herself, and I will not also lose my reputation and that of my son... because of *you*.

Dark thoughts began to gather in her mind, until she was forced to put on a professional smile when the shop bell rang gaily and a pair of chattering ladies bustled inside wishing good morning to *dear* 'Madame'.

After Shaw had recited Evening Prayer – a service attended only by himself and the verger – he and Mrs Shaw walked down the hill to the village hall. A small, squat building in the Arts and Crafts style, with pebble-dash walls and dark green Tudoresque beams, it had been built using money raised by public subscription, plus a large donation from the present Lord Addenham's father, whose name featured in large letters on the foundation stone.

It had been erected mainly to house the activities of the newly formed parish council, when the church had finally ceded the last of its powers of civil governance in 1894, but with the proviso that it would also be available for cultural and artistic activities. For this reason, it was the meeting place of the Lower Addenham Dramatic Society.

Shaw had never really been one for amateur theatricals. He had briefly been involved with the 'Footlights' theatrical club as an undergraduate in Cambridge, but had found it took too much time out of his studies. The theatre was a pleasant evening's distraction, he conceded, but he wished no more involvement than that; any secular play, he felt, would always fall short of the true drama of the Eucharist.

He was pleased that he would only be required to act as prompt for three performances; even that was a little more than he would have liked but as all he was required to do was to follow the script, he considered it no great hardship.

Upon entering the building the Shaws were met by the bustle and sense of expectation that anyone who has been involved in amateur theatrics will be familiar with. The hall, with its rows of rush-seated chairs and its little stage, was crowded with around two dozen people in various states of undress; the air was thick with cigarette smoke and the smell of greasepaint.

There was a loud hubbub of conversation, snatches of song and sounds of piano music, and the occasional crash and bang as something technical happened behind the stage. Shaw ducked as a step ladder was carried past him by two young men; his wife led him to the front of the hall.

'I'll introduce you to Mrs Bardell,' she said. 'She's the director'.

'Now darling,' came a stentorian female voice from behind the dark-red velvet curtains of the stage. 'Enter Hamlet.'

'She's in the middle of something from the sounds of it,' said Mrs Shaw as they stood by the stage. 'Let's just peep through and make sure to catch her at a good time.'

Mrs Shaw mounted the stage from a little stairway and looked through a chink in the centre of the curtains; Shaw stood beside here somewhat self-consciously, although they seemed to be completely unnoticed in the preparatory chaos around them.

'"Enter Hamlet",' roared the female voice. 'Where is he?'

Shaw then heard a man's voice. 'Ah…Mrs Bardell, it should be "enter Queen and Polonius". Hamlet does not enter for some time.'

'No, no, no, darling!' insisted the woman. 'It quite clearly says here in the script…Act Three, Scene Four…enter….yes, as I *said*, "enter Queen and Polonius". Now where is Hamlet? We need him for this scene. Hamlet, er Richard, darling, where are you?'

'It's Ronald,' said the man with a sigh, 'and he's not here yet.'

'All right everybody, five minute break!' announced the

woman with a gasp of frustration. 'Curtains. Curtains!'

Shaw stepped back and nearly fell off the stage as the curtains swept away suddenly, revealing a partially constructed set; a man was painting imitation stonework on plywood flats which Shaw assumed was meant to represent the castle of Elsinore.

'Darling Mrs Vicar!' exclaimed the stentorian woman, who stepped forward to embrace Mrs Shaw as if she were a long-lost daughter. She was of uncertain age – anywhere between 50 and 80, thought Shaw – with a heavily made up face, a flowing, artistic gown of what appeared to be pre-war vintage, and some sort of turban-like hat.

'And darling Mr Vicar!' she coo'd as she let Mrs Shaw go. Before Shaw could speak he felt his lips smothered by the woman's scented face-powder as she kissed him on the cheek; the general sensation, thought Shaw, was of having one's face pushed unexpectedly into a box of Turkish Delight.

'This is Mrs Bardell, our director,' said Mrs Shaw, as she discretely wiped her face with her handkerchief.

'Aren't we lucky to have you as Polonius?' she trilled.

The man next to her, dressed half in a medieval tunic and half in grey flannel trousers, sighed again. Despite the rather strange looking grey wig he wore, Shaw recognised him as one of the choristers from his church, Clarence Weekes.

'I'm Polonius, Mrs Bardell,' said Weekes.

'You're what, dear?' asked the director, looking at Weekes as if she had never seen him before.

'I said *I'm* playing Polonius; I believe the vicar is going to be our prompt.'

'He can't be the prompt darling, that's dear Mr Hawthorne,' said Mrs Bardell.

'Haw*trey*,' corrected Mrs Shaw. 'He's ill, you may recall.'

'Of course, of course,' said Mrs Bardell. 'And dear Mr Vicar is replacing him. Wonderful, wonderful!'

'Good evening Mr Shaw,' said Weekes. 'Thanks awfully for helping out at such short notice.'

'Not at all,' murmured Shaw, secretly wondering just what he had got himself into.

'I do not approve of prompts,' said Mrs Bardell airily. 'In the *professional* theatre, we rarely use them. Actors are expected to know their lines – to be, as dear Henry Irving used to say, "off the book" – before the first rehearsal even starts. But, well, with amateurs one must make exceptions I suppose…'

'Where do I sit?' asked Shaw.

'Oh, Polonius dear,' said Mrs Bardell, 'show Mr, er, show the gentleman here – the darling vicar – to the pit, there's a dear. Now I must speak to…where is Ophelia? Ophelia!'

Mrs Bardell looked to the back of the hall and then swayed down the stage steps and swept towards a group of young women gathered at the back of the hall, leaving only a lingering smell of perfume behind her.

'You'd better wait in the pit,' said Mrs Shaw. 'I must dash and see what Madame wants me to do. Lucky old you, you can just relax and smoke a pipe for the next hour.'

As his wife disappeared behind the stage, Shaw felt somewhat uneasy following the mention of the word 'pit', but it transpired this was simply a small partitioned off area at the foot of the stage, where he was to sit at a small table with a little electric lamp.

'It's just here,' said Weekes, leading the way down the stage steps. 'I expect you'll want to settle down and have a look at the script. We're having a tech first but then it's curtain up at 7.30.'

'A...tech?' asked Shaw.

'Yes, a technical rehearsal,' said Weekes. 'One or two things need to be ironed out in Act Three. Should have been done a long time ago, but well, you can see what we have to work with.' Weekes raised an eyebrow archly, looking in the direction of Mrs Bardell.

'Here's your script,' said Weekes, pointing to a tattered sixpenny edition of *Hamlet* on the table.

'I took the precaution of bringing my own,' said Shaw, raising a slim leather bound edition he had brought from his study.

'Won't be any good to you,' said Weekes. 'You'll need to use the official one as it has all the cues and so on in it. Quite a lot of the play's been cut as, well, some people' – here the eyebrow was raised again and the arch expression returned – 'some people find it all too much to learn. Hence the need for a prompt.'

'I see. I shall endeavour to do my best,' said Shaw.

'You can't be any worse than old Hawtrey,' said Weekes with a chuckle. 'Most of the time we had to end up prompting *him*. Well I must dash – I must find my dresser, he's the only one that truly understands the architecture of my hair.' Looking upwards, he patted his wig with a doubtful gesture and then was gone.

Shaw sat back and lit his pipe, affecting to look at the script but occasionally glancing around the hall. He recognised a number of people from the village and from his church, bustling around in preparation from the show, and received nods and waves from some of them.

'Technical rehearsal in ten minutes!' called Mrs Bardell as she strode from the back of the hall to the stage, and then disappeared behind it.

Shaw noticed that following the retreat of Mrs Bardell behind the stage, one woman in particular seemed to dominate the proceedings. A stout woman, to put it charitably, with strikingly red hair; she was speaking to young Mrs Cranston, the post-mistress. The latter woman was dressed in the flowing, medieval-style gown required for her role as Ophelia, Hamlet's potential wife.

'I'm sorry Mrs Hexham,' said Mrs Cranston with a trembling attempt at firmness, 'but Mrs Bardell definitely said she wanted to use the fake blood in Act Three.'

So this, thought Shaw, was the famous Mrs Hexham, alleged to be the writer of what the popular press called 'poison-pen letters'. He listened, while giving an appearance of being highly absorbed in prodding the contents of his pipe-bowl.

'Well,' sniffed Mrs Hexham, 'I don't like it. It will ruin Polonius' costume and that means we shall have that French...*person*...complaining as his tabard comes from her shop.'

Shaw noticed another woman approach the pair, a rather attractive dark-haired slim woman, somewhere between the end of youth and the beginning of middle age, dressed in a casual but elegant dress.

'That French person is Belgian,' she said through gritted teeth, glaring at Mrs Hexham.

'Forgive me, dear Madame,' oozed Mrs Hexham. 'It's just that so often these ladies who work in boutiques and...similar professions...*are* French. And usually Jewesses, though I'm sure I don't know why.'

'It is no matter,' said the woman. 'And I am not a Jewess.'

'*If* you say so,' said Mrs Hexham.

'I heard you mention the gown of Polonius,' said the Belgian woman. 'What is wrong with it?'

This, realised Shaw, must be Madame Dubois. It was clear there was an 'atmosphere' and the principal hostility seemed to emanate from Mrs Hexham, though she hid it well. He guessed the woman was well practised at deflecting blame.

'I was just saying,' trilled Mrs Hexham, 'that I'm sure you don't want Polonius' gown ruined by that silly imitation blood that…our director…wants thrown all over it.'

'*Au contraire,*' said Madame Dubois. 'I think it will be most dramatic and look, *tres effective* for the audience. It is no trouble to me as I have tested a small amount of the blood and it washes out easily.'

Mrs Hexham's face fell, but her affected smile soon returned. 'Of course you are right,' she said brightly. 'I always thought Mrs Bardell's idea about the blood was excellent, but I was merely concerned for your shop stock. After all, it's really nothing to do with me,' she sniffed.

'You're right,' said Mrs Cranston, 'it's *nothing to do with you.*'

Shaw noticed that the young woman had gone pale and was trembling slightly. Just at that moment, Madame Dubois put a protective arm around her.

'Come along Mrs *Cransonne,*' she said. 'Let us go to the dressing room and prepare our costumes.'

The Belgian woman glared at Mrs Hexham and led Mrs Cranston briskly behind the stage.

Mrs Hexham shrugged and directed her attention to a young man assembling some sort of spotlight near the stage.

'I don't think it should go there,' she said.

'Director said it's to be moved,' said the young man hesitatingly.

'It's *always* been on the *other side,*' insisted Mrs Hexham, looming over the hapless youth, who dropped a spanner onto the floor as he fumbled with the light.

'Right-oh,' he murmured wearily, perhaps unwilling to challenge the logical fallacy of Mrs Hexham's appeal to tradition, and began moving the apparatus to the opposite side of the stage.

Shaw frowned and re-lit his pipe. Our Lord, he reflected, had enjoined His followers to judge not, lest they themselves be judged, but it was hard not to feel somewhat judgemental towards Mrs Hexham. Even if he had not known of her history, he would have suspected her of being a bully based on the last few minutes alone.

The doors at the rear of the hall then creaked open and Shaw saw a young man whom he vaguely recognised saunter in. His parents, he believed, were occasionally at divine service but he had not seen the son in church before.

Handsome to an extent that even other men could notice, he was dressed in expensively cut tweeds and with a college scarf draped around his neck (Magdalen, thought Shaw, though being a Cambridge alumnus he was not well up on Oxford colours).

The youngster sauntered in as if he owned the place, puffing on a cigarette. He looked around the hall with an air of bored patrician ownership, and then ground his cigarette under his heel on the parquet floor.

'Evening ladies,' he said to a group of young women in various degrees of Tudor costume who were practicing a John Dowland song around the piano.

'You're not all changed yet,' he said, eyeing them up and down as he leaned against the instrument. 'I must say you look awfully good half in and half out of those costumes but I wish you'd make your minds up which half is going to succeed.'

The stern middle aged woman seated at the piano, whom Shaw vaguely recognised from the Mother's Union, snapped the keyboard lid shut.

'That's enough girls, you'd better get ready now. So should you, Mr Havering.'

She stood up and led the way as the young women swished past Havering. Shaw noticed that out of the group of four, three blushed and giggled as they passed, and one said 'Hello Ronnie!' coyly. One, however, simply glared balefully at him and swept past regally, in a manner fit for Queen Elizabeth herself.

Shaw, once again occupying himself by prodding his pipe, recognised the final woman as the group passed by him to go behind the stage. It was Gladys Kersey, the pretty young barmaid from the George. He wondered why she had cold-shouldered Havering. Perhaps, Shaw thought, as a barmaid she was immune to the charms of saloon-bar lotharios, though she seemed to display more than just professional indifference to Havering.

Shaw shrugged. It was not his business, and he returned to perusing the script.

'Evening vicar,' said the young man, pausing as he passed by Shaw. 'You've been roped in as well, I see.'

Shaw stood up slowly. 'Good evening, er, Mr Havering, I think?'

'That's right,' said Havering as they shook hands.

Shaw noticed the man had an air of confidence mixed with a certain immaturity, a combination which he had noticed in the younger generation of public-school men. The diffidence and stiff formality of his own generation seemed absent in today's youth, he reflected. A result of the Great War, perhaps, he mused, and then snapped out of his train of thought as he realised Havering had asked him a question.

'Ready for the tech, vicar?'

'The rehearsal?' replied Shaw, looking at his watch. 'Ah yes. I believe it is about to start in a few minutes.'

'Right-o,' said Havering, stepping up on to the stage. 'I'll just have a bit of a warm up.'

He took his scarf off and tossed it carelessly into the wings. He began pacing up and down, reeling off the play's most famous soliloquy with effortless ease.

> To be, or not to be, that is the question:
> Whether 'tis nobler in the mind to suffer
> The slings and arrows of outrageous fortune,
> Or to take arms against a sea of troubles
> And by opposing end them. To die—to sleep,
> No more;

He then paused and clutched his forehead dramatically, snapping his fingers in Shaw's direction.

'Come on vicar, line, line!' he said imperiously.

Shaw fumbled with the script and eventually found the correct scene.

'"...and by a sleep to say we end..."' he prompted.

'"...the heartache and the thousand tum tee tum tee tum tee tum,"' countered Havering. 'Yes, got it now. Look here though, you'll have to be quicker off on the mark than that if I dry tonight.'

'Dry?' asked Shaw.

'Yes, you know, forget my lines,' said Havering. 'I don't want anyone showing me up in front of that old…'

Here Havering caught himself and seemed to pay a token degree of respect to the presence of a clergyman so nearby.

'That old *trouper* Mrs Hexham. Wouldn't do to upset her, now would it?,' he asked sarcastically.

'I shall be on the mark,' said Shaw firmly, 'rest assured, should you "dry".'

'Good chap,' said Havering, turning away to face stage

left. 'Ah, talk of the devil, here she is. How do, Mrs H?'

As Mrs Hexham strode on to the stage, Shaw detected an immediate chilling of the atmosphere. The young man and the middle-aged woman regarded each other coldly for a moment in silence, a silence which was broken abruptly by Mrs Hexham, who, rather than acknowledge Havering, simply turned to shout up stage.

'Where is Mr Hexham? Has anyone seen my husband?' she barked.

'Probably deserted you if he's got any sense,' whispered Havering at a level audible only to Shaw.

'What was that?' queried Mrs Hexham, turning back to face the young actor.

'Let's hope this scene makes sense,' said Havering quickly. 'Your hubby's stage manager after all so if it all goes wrong it'll be his fault.'

'Everything will be perfectly all right,' sniffed Mrs Hexham, 'Mr Hexham and myself will ensure it is. It is a difficult technical scene and that is why Mrs Bardell kindly allowed me to be in charge of its direction.'

Havering simply rolled his eyes and then greeted, with relative cordiality, the other members of the cast who were to play in the scene: Weekes, as Polonius, Ophelia's father; and Madame Dubois as Hamlet's mother, Queen Gertrude.

'You should be in costume by now,' snapped Mrs Hexham at Havering.

'Oh dear,' said Havering frostily. 'Well you haven't got much time to find a stand-in so I'm afraid you'll have to put up with me just as I am.'

Shaw noticed a slight smile flick across Weekes' face at this remark; Madame Dubois remained impassive.

One of the young women members of the cast poked her head out from the wings and called across to Mrs Hexham.

'Mr Hexham's on his way,' she said, and then retreated.

'*Here* he is,' said Mrs Hexham with exasperation, as a timid looking man emerged from behind the castle scenery at the back of the stage. 'Where on earth have you been?'

'Sorry,' murmured the man. 'Bit of technical work needing doing and I can't find Bert. Said he'd help.'

'Bert Cranston – what do you need a half-trained stage hand for?' exclaimed Mrs Hexham, her voice rising in pitch. 'This all should have been done weeks ago. Really, if you can't get this sort of thing right I wish you wouldn't bother.'

Shaw winced inwardly with embarrassment at the man receiving such a brow-beating from his wife, especially in front of others.

Hexham, however, merely shrugged. 'Shall we get started?' he said.

'*We* are all ready to start, no thanks to you,' said Mrs Hexham. She turned to the assembled cast members.

'As you know, this is Act Three, scene four; the Queen's Closet. Are you with us, Mr Shaw? I hope you will not be required, but, well, with…this company…one never knows.'

Shaw fumbled with the script until he found his place. 'I have it,' he exclaimed.

'Then perhaps we can get started?' said Mrs Hexham with a sigh. 'Now, Polonius is hiding behind the curtain, or the arras, as it says in the script. Hamlet thinks it is his enemy, King Claudius, and stabs at him…'

There was a crash as the doors at the back of the hall opened and a man strode in, knocking one of the chairs aside as he did so. Shaw recognised him immediately; it was Bert Cranston, the man upon whom he had inadvertently eavesdropped that morning. He felt his stomach tighten as he realised an unpleasant scene was imminent.

'Ah, *dear* Mr Cranston,' said Mrs Hexham with icy coolness as the man approached the stage. 'So glad you could join us at last. Shall we begin?'

Cranston glared at Mrs Hexham, but brushed past her and stood next to her husband upstage by the painted castle walls.

'Polonius is behind the curtain,' said Mrs Hexham. 'Why aren't you behind the curtain, Mr Weekes?' she asked.

'Because there isn't a curtain,' said Weekes in a tired voice.

'Reginald, why isn't the curtain ready?' snapped Mrs Hexham at her husband. 'Really I've had enough of this sloppiness! It's curtain up in less than two hours.'

'Curtain up and we've no curtain,' quipped Havering dryly, as he lit a cigarette.

Mrs Hexham coughed theatrically and waved imaginary smoke away from her face. 'Disgusting habit. I keep saying cigarettes ought to be banned from the hall. ' She then cast a glance at Shaw. 'And pipes,' she sniffed. 'Can we please have the curtain put up?'

Hexham and Cranston began pulling a large white curtain from the wings across the stage on a wire, so that it hung about two feet downstage from the painted scenery of the castle walls. It was about six feet across and seven feet high, covering the stage left exit. The two men tweaked and pulled it until it resembled something like a window curtain.

'It looks like a painter's dust-sheet,' snapped Mrs Hexham. 'What happened to the one we used before?'

'That big heavy one?' said Weekes. 'Apparently it all started falling to bits so it's being repaired. Won't be ready in time though so we'll have to make do with this one tonight.'

'Ridiculous,' said Mrs Hexham 'but I suppose it will

have to do.' She glanced down at her script. 'Polonius is behind the curtain. Start from Hamlet's line. "Now mother, what's the matter?".'

Weekes sighed and stood behind the curtain; Madame Dubois reclined on a shabby chaise longue a few feet away from it. Havering approached his fictional mother.

'"Now mother…"'

'Wait,' said Madame Dubois, standing up. 'We are supposed to embrace.'

'I don't see why,' said Mrs Hexham. 'It's not in the script.'

'Shakespeare hardly ever puts directions in his scripts,' said Madame Dubois, 'but I feel it is right for them to embrace at this point. To show how much Hamlet loves his mother.'

'I still don't see why we have to have all this hugging,' sniffed Mrs Hexham.

'She fancies Ronnie, that's why!' came an unidentified voice from the wings; it was followed by a bawdy chorus of male laughter.

'Quiet!' snapped Mrs Hexham. 'Very well then, if you *must*,' she said.

Madame Dubois stood and clasped her arms around Havering, and then returned to her seat. The scene continued, as Havering rattled off his lines peremptorily.

'"Come, come and sit you down,"' he said, '"you shall not budge, you go not till I set you up a glass where you may see the inmost part of you."'

'"What wilt tou do?"' replied Madame Dubois.

'It's *thou*, Madame,' interrupted Mrs Hexham. 'Thou, thou. Not "tou". Can't you get that right?'

'I find it difficult,' hissed Madame Dubois. 'Maybe you would find the same if you spoke a play in French.'

'Oh come on, for heaven's sake,' said Havering wearily.

'What does it matter if she's got an accent? We're all supposed to be Danish in this play anyway!'

'Shakespeare was English,' sniffed Mrs Hexham. 'Proper enunciation of the words is important. Oh well, carry on.'

'"Thou wilt not murder me?"' exclaimed Madame Dubois, correctly pronouncing 'thou' this time. '"Help, help, ho!"'

'"What ho! Help, help, help!"' called Weekes in response from behind the curtain.

'Where's the blasted dagger?' said Havering, looking around the stage.

'Here you are,' said Cranston, stepping out of the wings and holding up a large knife in front of Havering. 'Got it working a treat now.'

'Thanks Bert,' said Havering. 'Show me how it works, will you?'

'I don't approve of this,' said Mrs Hexham, 'I think it's overly melodramatic.'

'I thought you agreed to it,' said Havering. 'After all it was your husband's idea.'

'I think it's silly,' sniffed Mrs Hexham. 'But who am I to question these things, after all I have *no* authority here.' She looked away with a martyred expression.

Really, thought Shaw, mustering as much charity as he could, this was a tiresome woman, and he was glad he would only have to work with her briefly.

'Knife works like this, see,' said Hexham, stepping forward and taking the weapon from Cranston. 'It was my idea but Bert here did all the technical work. It's an ordinary kitchen knife. He's added a guard to make it look sort of medieval, and he's dulled the blade so's it can't do any damage.'

He rubbed the palm of his hand up and down the gleaming blade and pressed its point into his flesh, which remained unmarked.

'And here's the really clever bit,' said Hexham. 'He's hollowed out the wooden handle and put a spring inside, so when Hamlet stabs Polonius through the curtain, the blade won't do any harm but to the audience, it will look like it's gone into something.'

Here he demonstrated by thrusting the blade into Cranston's stomach and then withdrawing it. Shaw gasped at the realism of it. Cranston's face remained impassive.

'Well done,' said Havering. 'Looks jolly realistic. Ought to shake the audience out of their slumbers.'

'Well I think it's silly and over complicated,' said Mrs Hexham. 'We could have saved this fuss and just stabbed a real knife into a cushion held up behind the curtain, like I suggested.'

'That's all right for you to suggest,' said Weekes, looking out from behind the curtain, 'but it would be me holding the cushion and I don't quite trust Mr Havering's aim.'

'I couldn't care less about the silly thing,' said Mrs Hexham. 'He'll have to "stab" *me* anyway, not Mr Weekes, as I will be standing in front of him sprinkling that ridiculous imitation blood on the curtain.'

'Right-oh,' chuckled Havering as he stubbed his cigarette out on the floor and kicked the stub off the stage. 'Don't worry Weekes, I've no desire to stab *you*, old chap.' Here he looked pointedly at Mrs Hexham, whose expression remained blank.

'Anyway,' snapped Mrs Hexham, 'as discussed, I will enter from stage left, concealed by the curtain. Hamlet will stab me with the retractable knife, and then I will throw the theatrical blood over the curtain and Polonius' clothing before he emerges. It's all rather too tawdry for my liking, but it's nothing to do with me.'

'So you remind us, often,' said Madame Dubois.

'I still don't see why you have to be standing next to me,' said Weekes, somewhat tetchily. 'I'm quite capable of throwing imitation blood on myself.'

'As I said before,' said Mrs Hexham through gritted teeth, 'you won't be able to see it on your jacket properly from looking down. It has to be done by someone else or it will end up on the floor. I'd rather it wasn't me but anyone else is liable to make an awful mess.'

Shaw noticed that Weekes did not reply, but looked away from Mrs Hexham, pursing his lips and glancing heavenward.

'May we hurry?' said Madame Dubois. 'There is not much time before, how do you say, the curtain is up.'

'Come along then,' said Havering, taking the knife from Hexham and testing the blade on his hand a couple of times. Mrs Hexham stepped behind the curtain next to Weekes, and Havering approached them.

'"How now, a rat!"' he exclaimed. '"Dead for a ducat, dead!"'

He thrust the dagger into the curtain, angling it so that the blade's movement against the outline of Mrs Hexham's body could clearly be seen from the audience's perspective. Shaw noticed a glint of red as some paste jewels stuck to the hilt caught one of the stage lights.

'I can't see any blood on the curtain,' said Havering. 'I thought that was the whole point.'

'I'm not using it yet,' said Mrs Hexham. 'We only have one sheet to use as a curtain. It has to be washed out each night – by me, of course, – as does Polonius' costume and I am not wasting...'

'Yes, yes, all right,' interrupted Havering. 'Hang on, Weekes, I'll give you the line again. '"Dead for a ducat, dead!"'

Weekes staggered out from behind the curtain, clutching

his chest and overacting somewhat, thought Shaw.

'"Oh!"' he wailed. '"I am slain!"'

'"Falls and dies",' said Mrs Hexham, emerging from behind the the curtain, as Weekes collapsed theatrically on the floor.

'Very well, I suppose that will have to do,' she continued. She then put a hand to her forehead. 'I must go and rest for a bit before curtain up. I can feel one of my headaches coming on.'

'Oh Lord,' said Mr Hexham, without much enthusiasm, and followed after his wife as she left the stage.

As Mrs Hexham departed, Shaw noticed that the four people left on stage – Cranston, Weekes, Havering and Madame Dubois – were all regarding her with what appeared to be looks of bitter resentment.

Chapter Three

There was an interlude of an hour which gave Shaw and his wife just enough time to return home and eat the cold supper left out for them by Hettie, and then they returned to the village hall in time for 'curtain up' at 7.30.

'I'm awfully glad there wasn't a scene,' whispered Mrs Shaw as they entered the hall, which was now beginning to fill up with audience members.

'A scene? Surely one expects that in a theatre?' said Shaw.

'You know what I mean, Lucian,' chided Mrs Shaw. 'Between Mr Cranston and Mrs Hexham. I saw from the wings when he arrived on the stage and I wondered if there was going to be the most almighty row about those horrible letters, but everyone seemed to stay calm.'

'Yes,' mused Shaw, 'he did seem calm. I wonder...I suspect perhaps everyone is reserving their energy for the performance, and after that there may be a frank exchange of views. Mrs Hexham, of course, can simply deny any knowledge of the letters as they were unsigned; it will be difficult to prove her involvement.'

'Hush, here she comes now,' whispered Mrs Shaw.

Mrs Hexham bustled past them. 'You're late,' she snapped. Curtain up in five minutes.'

Shaw raised an eyebrow at his wife, who raised both of hers in return, and then hurried off to assist with the dressing backstage.

Shaw took up his post at the foot of the stage and switched on the little electric lamp which gave just enough light for him to see the script in front of him on the table. From beyond the closed stage curtains he could just make out Mrs Bardell's voice from backstage, giving the cast some sort of pep-talk, which ended with the words 'attack, darlings! That's what acting *is*. Attack, attack!'

Shaw smiled to himself, thinking how odd the life of a professional actor must be; he felt somewhat glad he had never inclined to that world himself. From what he had seen of actors and actresses many of them seemed rather fraught, over-emotional people; it was not his sort of thing at all.

He realised the last time he had been involved in anything remotely theatrical was as part of the chorus in an officers' camp concert behind the lines at Cambrai in 1917; but that had been a jolly, back-slapping affair of camaraderie and high spirits; there was no inclination for off-stage drama and back-biting among those actors, when sudden, violent death was always an imminent possibility.

There would have been no poison-pen letters in the trenches either, he reflected grimly. Had anyone attempted such a preposterous act, he would have been summarily beaten – or worse – by his fellows.

Shaw looked around and saw the hall was almost full now with village folk, most of them youngsters got up in their Sunday best and chattering excitedly. Friends of the cast, he assumed, or perhaps those who wanted a cheaper alternative to the 'pictures', which required outlay on bus or train fares to Great Netley.

The stern female pianist entered the hall and sat down at her instrument opposite Shaw; and the chattering diminished somewhat. A crescendo of notes was played and then there was an almighty rumbling, scraping and shuffling sound as the audience rose to its feet for a brisk rendition of *God Save the King*.

The raggedly-sung anthem ended, the house lights dimmed and the audience sat back down as the curtains opened with a creaking sound of insufficiently-oiled pulley wheels.

The play opened with a scene on the castle walls of Elsinore, as two guards patrolled at night. There was some tittering and whispering in the audience; Shaw heard a woman in the front row say to her companion proudly 'That's our Cyril!'

Shaw was required to prompt several times during the opening scene, resulting in more giggling from the audience, which did not bode well, he thought. He realised he had to keep his eyes both on what was happening on stage and on the page in front of him, which with the pool of dim light cast by the lamp, was a difficult task.

When, however, the ghost of Hamlet's father the king appeared, the actors managed to get through the scene without forgetting their lines; perhaps it was just stage fright wearing off, thought Shaw. He had to admit the scene was rather impressive, with the actor playing the king dusted all over with flour to appear white, and some sort of theatrical smoke drifting in from the wings, wafted by Bert Cranston using a large piece of cardboard as a fan.

This held the audience's attention for while but as the play wore on, it was clear that boredom was beginning to set in, despite the shortening of many of the long speeches. Most of the actors, thought Shaw, really were not very good and read their lines woodenly, sometimes even bumping into the scenery or tripping over their unfamiliar costumes as they entered and exited, provoking more tittering from the audience.

The only members of the cast with any noticeable skill, he thought, were Mrs Cranston as Ophelia, Madame Dubois as the Queen, Weekes as Polonius and Havering as Hamlet; none of them required prompting nor missed any cues or entries.

Havering pronounced the famous 'to be or not to be' soliloquy with consummate ease, although he was put off slightly by a farmhand in the second row saying audibly 'that is the question' in response to the opening line; there was some giggling in the audience when his friend next to him then was heard to ask ''ow did you know that?'

Then came Act Three, Scene Four, where Hamlet was to stab Polonius behind the curtain. Shaw realised the interval was scheduled for after this scene, and found himself thinking longingly of a cup of tea (the hall was not licensed for the sale of alcohol).

After Weekes, as Polonius, had concealed himself behind the curtain, there was some sniggering in the audience as Hamlet and his mother embraced, but then a collective intake of breath after the cue of 'Dead for a ducat, dead!' as Havering raised the dagger and plunged it into the curtain.

There was a cry of pain followed by an audible gasp from the audience. Then a pause; Shaw wondered when the false bloodstain would appear on the sheet, but nothing could be seen other than a small dark patch where the knife had gone through the sheet. Havering appeared frozen to the spot, the dagger still clenched in his fist, and when his eyes met Shaw's briefly he saw panic in them.

Had someone forgotten a line?, thought Shaw. He had been transfixed by the scene and had not been paying attention. He glanced hurriedly at the script; Polonius was supposed to emerge from behind the curtain. Where was he?

There was a clatter as Havering looked down at the now bloodied knife in his hand and dropped it on the stage.

Shaw decided to risk it and opened his mouth to prompt Weekes with 'I am slain', but before he could do so, there was a tearing sound followed by a crash as the curtain was pulled down and a figure fell forward with a sickening thud onto the boards.

That did not seem to be the way they had rehearsed the scene, thought Shaw, but the low angle with a spotlight close by made it difficult for him to make out exactly what was going on. There was concerned whispering and muttering from the audience and then a woman in the front row screamed 'she's dead!'

Shaw tentatively stood up to get a better view of the stage floor, and realised that it was not Polonius that lay prostrate on the boards, but Mrs Hexham.

Fred Arbon was bored. He was seated near the back of the hall and could not see the stage properly due to the woman in front of him wearing a large hat, which did not help matters. He would rather have been at the pictures, or enjoying a drink or two at the George, but his sweetheart, Iris Garrod, was playing a lady-in-waiting and he felt duty bound to support her.

As the newly appointed regular village constable, he now had a good wage, living quarters and a bicycle to ride around on; he was doing much better than he had been as a farmhand and it seemed the next logical step was to get married, and he did not want a falling out with Iris before he managed to put the question to her.

He fingered his collar and tie awkwardly and undid the

buttons on his new suit jacket; he was not used to wearing one except on Sundays. That was another advantage of the job, though, he thought to himself.

Before he retired the last village bobby had told him a good wrinkle; get a tailor to make a suit jacket in the same blue serge cloth as the regulation police trousers. Then for off-duty clothing, all you needed to do was buy a jacket and a collar and a tie, as everything else – boots, trousers and shirt – was provided free as part of the uniform, and they were the bits that wore out the quickest. No Sunday best nor wedding suit required – it all meant more money in the Post Office, thought Arbon with a smile of satisfaction.

The play had started out well enough, he thought, what with the ghost appearing on stage like that in clouds of smoke; almost as good as the pictures, that was. But then it had just seemed to be a lot of long speeches in old fashioned language, like the prayers in church, and not much happening. He began to long for a pint of mild in the George and hoped that there would be enough time to get one in – as well as, with any luck, a bit of a goodnight kiss in Lover's Lane – before he had to walk Iris home to her parents' cottage.

Arbon directed his attention back to the stage. Hello, he thought – things seemed to be picking up a bit. The prince fellow – Hamlet – had drawn a knife and was about to stab the old boy, the one that droned on all the time – Poe something – behind the curtain.

Now how, thought Arbon, is he going to manage that without hurting someone? Stop the dagger just short of the curtain, he assumed, or stab just outside the shape of the chap standing behind it. But no! Arbon saw the dagger plunge deep into the curtain. Then nothing seemed to happen for a moment, until there was an almighty crash, the curtain fell down and a woman collapsed on the stage.

Arbon knew something was wrong right away, because the woman was not wearing old-time clothing, but a modern frock, and there was blood on it. The way she had fallen down did not look like play-acting either. Others in the audience had noticed too, although some seemed oblivious, as if it was all part of the tale.

Then something happened that snapped him out of it and spurred him into action. There was a scream from somewhere up front and a woman called out 'she's dead!' Then the young fellow – Hamlet – looked down at the dagger, dropped it on the stage and rushed down the little steps at the front, across to the exit doors and crashed through them.

All hell broke loose; there was yelling and shouts of 'fetch a doctor' and 'bring the curtains down'. Arbon realised somebody had to take charge. He fumbled for his whistle – which he kept on his person even when off duty, and blew a long blast on it. This seemed to bring a bit of hush, and he called out in a loud voice.

'Everybody stay in this hall. Nobody is to leave.'

Looking around him he saw a familiar face – Reverend Shaw – at the front of the hall, and he addressed him.

'Vicar, will you see to that? And get that front curtain down. Don't allow anyone on the stage.'

Shaw nodded in assent. Arbon ran to the exit doors and on the way, grabbed the young man operating the spotlight, whom he recognised as one of his fellow bell-ringers from church. 'Tom Pipe, you run and fetch the doctor and on the way find Reg Tanner, the special constable, in the police house. He'll be there as it's my night off. Got that?'

'Righto Fred!' nodded the boy, and dashed off.

Normally Arbon would have chided the youth for using

his Christian name to address him while on duty, but there was no time. He ran to the exit doors, picking his way through the audience, which was now milling around in a state of confusion. The last thing he heard as he left the building was the vicar's voice, with a note of authority he had not heard before, appealing for calm and for everyone to return to their seats.

Once outside, the bitter evening cold hit him like a splash of water. His eyes adjusted to the dark and he looked around to see if he could get a glimpse of that Hamlet fellow. He wondered if he should have stayed to keep people off the stage and so on, but decided that catching that young chap was more important – why on earth had he run off like that? Panic at having caused a serious accident, he assumed, but what if there was more to it?

His thought process was arrested when he caught sight of a flash of white – the colour of tunic that Hamlet had been wearing – over in the field opposite the hall. He peered into the gloom and in a beam of moonlight, saw it was the man he wanted. He blew his whistle again, in the hope he could get up a hue and cry from any passers by, and set off in pursuit.

'You there, stop!' he called as he neared the actor; the man turned to look at him briefly but kept on running.

The young man was not able to outrun Arbon, a keen footballer and expert batsman, who also kept his cigarette consumption to a minimum. The field was waterlogged and coated with thick mud; before long his quarry was exhausted and Arbon merely had to pick his way through the mud towards him and then clap a firm hand on his shoulder.

'Come along now,' he said sternly. 'I think the show's over for tonight, don't you?'

Detective Chief Inspector George Ludd, of the Midchester Criminal Investigation Department, sat back in his armchair and looked around him at the room, not quite able to take it all in.

He had moved a few weeks ago, and everything was now finally unpacked and in its proper place. He still could not really believe it. Their old pictures and things – the prints of the *Laughing Cavalier* and *When Did You Last See Your Father?* the porcelain ducks flying across the wall, the wedding photographs of his two girls, were all the same, but they looked smaller in the larger room with its big curving bay window and little shelf that went all around the room below the ceiling.

He was not quite sure what *that* was for, but Mrs Ludd said it was for putting ornamental brass plates or pewter tankards on, and so he made a mental note to have a look for some at Baldwin's department store the next chance he got.

It was daft, really, he thought, getting a bigger house when they did not need the space, but since his promotion to Chief Inspector he had more money coming in, and this was his chance to finally get a bigger garden for his hobby of vegetable growing.

He could, of course, have got an allotment instead, but he did not fancy that somehow. He did not think he would be able to sleep well at night knowing that his potential prize-winning vegetables were sitting unguarded. He had visions of legions of unemployed tramps marching down from the north and turning his plot into a feeding station.

They had found a house to rent on the new bypass on

the edge of Midchester; a house so new that nobody else had lived in it. Semi-detached, with dark green Tudor beams on the gable and one of those wooden gates with a rising sun design on it; a front garden almost the size of his old back garden, and a back garden twice the size of that.

There was even a garage, with green double doors and matching Tudor beams above them; and that had caused him to make his most reckless purchase in many a year: a nearly-new Austin Sixteen motor car.

After all, he thought, there was no point having a garage without something to put in it; and anyway, it was too far to walk to the police station now, there was no bus service that way and it would hardly be fitting for a man in his position to ride a bicycle to work.

He could hear his wife humming as she tidied away the supper things in the little kitchen next door. It was good to see her happy even though he knew she was lonely away from her old neighbours; she was, however, trying to make new friends and was even talking about changing her allegiance from the Methodist chapel in town to the large, red-brick Anglican church up the road. A better class of Christians, she said.

Ludd did not have much concern for that, preferring the pub to the church on Sundays except for high days and holidays, but he had noticed an improvement in the availability of local watering holes.

His old local pub had been a slightly down-at-heel Victorian corner bar; people always seemed to go quiet and turn away when he walked in. Here, however, there was a large, Elizabethan style roadhouse – The Haywain – with hunting prints on the walls, table service, and a clientele that seemed to view him as something approaching a respected member of the community.

He smiled in satisfaction at his lot in life, and turned up

the gas on the fire next to him. He wondered whether they might even afford a skivvy; after all there was a spare room for one, but then there was precious little work to do in a house like this – gas fires, even in the bedrooms if you please – a hot water geyser in the kitchen and some unfathomable electrical contraption that did the weekly washing. Ah well, he thought, no rush.

Before he could sink back into his armchair, he heard the tinkling of the telephone bell from the hallway. He went to answer it; Mrs Ludd still distrusted the instrument, despite having had one in their old house for a year or two. He expected it would be Mr Waller on the line, President of the Midchester Horticultural Society, calling to discuss his application for membership.

He stopped himself just in time from saying the name of his old house's exchange, and instead pronounced 'Highcroft 6174'. He prepared to greet Mr Waller cordially. Ought he to risk calling him Waller, he wondered, or would that be considered forward? He wasn't quite sure how formal they were at the Horticultural Society. Perhaps keep the 'Mr' just in case, he thought.

His smile turned to a frown as he listened, and he realised, sullenly, that he had been proud before a fall. It was the station, and his presence was urgently required.

'Everybody please remain calm,' said Shaw, standing up and walking to the foot of the stage. The actors seemed frozen in position, all staring in horror at the body of Mrs Hexham. Shaw realised from one glance she was dead, but did not wish to alarm the audience further.

'Close the curtains please,' he called upstage, and this

was duly done, but unfortunately Mrs Hexham's upper body remained visible. Shaw moved the curtains so that she was covered and turned to the audience. He could tell that panic was rising and he wished to avoid a stampede for the exits.

'There has been a most unfortunate accident,' he said loudly and firmly. The noise level in the hall dropped, and he realised he 'had the floor' for perhaps a few moments.

'Constable Arbon,' he continued, 'has instructed that nobody leave the hall. Would the ticket sellers kindly ensure this order is carried out?' He looked doubtfully at the two elderly ladies selling tickets at a card table by the door, but one of them nodded and stood up to lock the main exit.

'Is she dead?' called a man from the back of the hall.

Shaw did not wish to cause further consternation and avoided the question. 'If there is any doctor or medical man in the house,' he said, 'would he please come forward?'

He strained his eyes but could not see anybody he knew; Doctor Holt, the local physician, was certainly not there. Then a timid looking middle aged woman in a cloche hat approached the stage.

'I'm a nurse at the cottage hospital,' she said in a low voice. 'May I be of any assistance?'

Shaw spoke loudly. 'Thank you nurse, kindly assist Mrs Hexham behind the stage.' Then as he led her towards the stage steps, he added in a low voice, 'I am certain she is dead, but did not wish to announce this. Would you please stay with her until Constable Arbon returns, and assist any of the cast who may be feeling faint?'

'Yes of course,' whispered the woman, and Shaw noticed her initial timidity had been replaced by a professional confidence. He parted the curtain slightly to let her through, then turned to the audience.

'Perhaps we might have a moment of quiet prayer,' he announced, and bowed his head. He then recited from memory the Collect for Aid Against All Perils from the order for Evening Prayer:

'Lighten our darkness we beseech thee O Lord, and by thy great mercy defend us from all perils and dangers of this night, for the love of thy only son our saviour Jesus Christ. Amen'.

There were a few murmured 'amens' but then low talking began again, increasing in volume, and the same man shouted out from the back of the hall. 'She's dead I'll wager,' followed by 'hush!' from the woman next to him.

Shaw breathed a sigh of relief when the side exit doors opened and Constable Arbon entered. His boots and trouser bottoms were caked with mud; he was holding lightly on to the arm of Havering, whose costume was coated in filth. Behind them came another police constable, this one in uniform. The volume of chatter in the hall suddenly dropped and all eyes were fixed on the door.

'Right then,' said Arbon in a loud voice. 'As I said, nobody's to leave just for now. Special Constable Tanner here will make sure of that, while I go backstage with this...gentleman.'

'What's going on?' called a woman from close by. 'Is that woman dead? It's Mrs Hexham, ain't it? What did that young feller run off for?'

This was followed by a chorus of questions which Arbon placated by raising his free hand.

'All in good time, ladies and gentlemen,' he said. 'Now take your places *please*. Constable Tanner has already telephoned to Midchester for reinforcements so we'll let you go just as soon as ever we can.'

Shaw stepped forward. 'Has Doctor Holt been

summoned?' he asked Tanner.

'Sorry vicar,' said Tanner. 'His wife says he's delivering a baby out Netley way, not expected back for some time. No telephone there, neither.'

'Very well,' said Shaw. 'Fortunately we have a nurse attending to Mrs Hexham. I have sent her on to the stage. Shall you require me to remain here?'

'If you'd kindly come with me, Mr Shaw,' said Arbon, 'I'd like to speak with you and the others backstage. Back to your places now everybody please,' he added sternly, 'or you'll be on a charge of obstruction.'

Shaw nodded and cleared a way through the crowd of people who were now reluctantly returning to their seats. Havering remained quiet, looking down at the floor, as Arbon escorted him through the little door at the side of the proscenium to the back-stage area.

'You sit down there young sir,' he said to Havering, pointing to a row of chairs by the side of the stage, 'and don't you move. You're in my line of sight so don't try running off again unless you want to be handcuffed. And you lot' – here he indicated a gaggle of cast members who had emerged from the curtained off area referred to as the 'dressing rooms' – 'you stay put until I call for you.'

Arbon stepped up on stage and looked at Mrs Hexham's body.

'You the nurse, miss?' he asked to the woman hovering next to the corpse.

'Yes,' said the nurse. 'Miss James.'

'Dead, ain't she?' he asked.

'Yes,' replied Miss James. 'A stab wound of some sort. At a guess I'd say the heart has been penetrated. It must have been a terrible accident.'

'Murdered more like,' said Hexham suddenly. He was standing upstage and looking at his wife's corpse with a blank expression on his face . 'Someone murdered her.'

'If you would only speak when spoken to sir,' said Arbon, 'we'll get along much more easily. Let's leave the speculation until the detectives arrive.'

'Now,' continued the constable, 'the knife wound was done by that there dagger, I suppose.' He pointed with the muddied toe of his boot to the weapon which lay next to Mrs Hexham, unmoved since Havering had dropped it.

Weekes, who looked visibly shaken, stepped forward from the wings and addressed the policeman.

'How on earth did it happen?' he quavered. 'The knife was a dummy.' He leaned down to pick up the object but his arm was grabbed by Arbon.

'*Don't* do that sir,' he urged, gently pushing Weekes back. 'That's evidence, that is. Only for the police to touch.'

'Then will you please hurry?' said Madame Dubois, who was pale but composed. 'I do not wish to remain next to this…body…any longer than I have to. I did not like her company when she was alive and I like it even less now she is dead.'

Arbon drew himself up to his full height and addressed the assembled cast.

'Now see here,' he said. 'I'm still hoping this was all just an accident but to be on the safe side, things has to be done through the proper channels. So myself and Special Constable Tanner will be taking statements from everybody on stage and in the hall, starting with them as was nearest the deceased. I'm sorry if that's an inconvenience to you, but this all has to be done proper, as I'm sure the vicar will tell you, him having had some experience of this sort of thing.'

Shaw cleared his throat, somewhat embarrassed at being made the centre of attention. 'Quite,' he said. 'Constable Arbon I am sure will be as quick as he can.'

'Thank you Mr Shaw,' said Arbon, looking at his wristwatch.

'If you'll be so kind as to wait patiently until my superiors arrive,' he continued, 'we'll all get along nicely, but I think we can all forget any ideas of a pint in the George this evening.'

Chief Inspector Ludd steered his car hesitantly through the pitch-black country lanes that led from Midchester to Lower Addenham. He enjoyed being able to drive himself instead of having to rely on a police car and driver, but found these back lanes a chore; the Austin's powerful headlamps seemed to do little to dispel the Stygian gloom. At least there was no fog, he thought to himself.

He had stopped off on the way to pick up a somewhat reluctant Detective Sergeant James McPherson who had been looking forward to spending the evening at home with his new wife.

He was a reliable man with whom he had worked on a previous case in the same village, and so was the natural choice to assist him. He looked to his right and saw McPherson's pale, angular features and reddish hair partly obscured by the brim of his trilby hat and dimly illuminated in the yellow light from the car's instrument panel.

Ludd briefly adjusted his own hat, feeling the unfamiliar soft felt of his new trilby. His wife had persuaded him to buy it, saying his bowler was old fashioned and made him look like a debt collector.

The younger detective offered a cigarette to his senior,

who declined it with a shake of his head; he found smoking a distraction from the effort of double de-clutching on some of the tricky bends in the road.

'Nice car this, sir,' observed McPherson.

'Pride and joy, lad,' said Ludd. 'Keep your eyes open for signs to Lower Addenham,' he added. 'I think it's this way but who can tell in this blasted dark?'

'Lower Addenham, eh?' said McPherson, after taking a deep drag on his cigarette. 'Didn't think we'd be back there so soon.'

'Nearly two years ago, that case you and I worked on,' said Ludd. 'And that was a double murder. From what the village bobby told me on the telephone this is just some unfortunate accident – someone got themselves killed during some amateur theatricals.'

'What are we being dragged out there for then?' asked McPherson.

'Duty officer at the station said something about a man running from the scene. Village bobby reckoned it might be a bit more than just an accident.'

'Och, probably all just a fancy,' chided McPherson. 'They had those murders there a couple of years ago, and that was the most exciting thing happened to them since, since the Relief o' Ladysmith. Maybe thinking there's murderers lurking round every corner.'

Ludd grunted non-committally. 'Duty officer says the village bobby's new,' he continued. 'Probably just worried about doing everything by the book, so we have to get roped in.'

'Let's hope we can get things sorted out quickly then,' said McPherson, throwing his cigarette out of the window.

'You only smoked half of that,' chided Ludd. 'You'll have to be more careful with money now you're married, you know. The lady wife will want her housekeeping.'

'Aye, I suppose you're right, sir,' replied McPherson. 'Jean's good with money, and maybe I should be more careful mysel'.'

'You're the Scot, not her,' said Ludd. 'It's supposed to come natural to your lot.'

McPherson frowned and Ludd wondered if he had been a little too personal.

'I'm no spendthrift,' said McPherson, 'but these digs we've had since we've been wed, och, the price is over too high. Heaven knows how we'll cope when any bairns come along.'

'Hmm,' replied Ludd. 'Digs do seem a lot these days. Our rent is a pretty penny as well. We'll have to take in a lodger before long,' he joked.

The car headlights picked out a black-and-white painted finger post at a junction. Ludd squinted at it, and then steered the car on to the main road into Lower Addenham.

Chapter Four

Shaw felt a sense of relief when he saw the two detectives walk into the village hall. The crowd was becoming restless and he did not think mild-mannered Special Constable Tanner would be able to hold them there much longer; and a mass refusal to obey the orders of a policeman would not be conducive to good relations between the police and public.

He recalled seeing in the illustrated newspapers a few years previously how one lone mounted policeman had held back a crowd of thousands at an association football match; but he doubted PC Tanner had the same authority and he certainly lacked a horse.

The new arrivals, however, had a natural air of leadership about them as they strode to the front of the hall, followed somewhat meekly by PC Tanner. The older detective climbed on to the stage and looked briefly through the curtain, then spoke briefly to Tanner, who fumbled in his pocket and handed over his truncheon.

The detective took the weapon and banged it several times on the stage with a thunderous crash; the crowd fell silent and he returned the wooden instrument to Tanner who tucked it away again in his pocket.

'Thank you for your patience ladies and gentlemen,' said the man. 'Everyone who was in the audience may now go home. Make sure you give your names and addresses to the constable at the door. We'll let you know if we need to speak to you.'

There was a flurry of questions from the audience regarding Mrs Hexham's condition, but the detective brushed this away with a blunt 'you'll be made aware of that in due course. Go home.'

Shaw watched as the younger detective assisted PC Tanner in herding the audience out of the front and side doors of the hall. Now that he had studied their faces, he realised who they were; recognition was mutual.

'I thought I might find you here,' said the older detective.

'Chief Inspector Ludd,' said Shaw. 'We seem destined to meet only in unfortunate circumstances.'

'Unfortunate circumstances is our bread and butter,' said Ludd. 'I thought to myself if something's happened in Lower Addenham, Reverend Shaw will know what's what. How are you, sir?'

'Very well, Chief Inspector. I trust you are well also?'

'Fair to middling,' grunted Ludd. 'You'll remember McPherson here.'

'Indeed,' said Shaw, bowing to McPherson. 'I am hardly likely to forget a man to whom I owe my life.'

The Scotsman merely nodded.

'Of course,' said Ludd. 'It was McPherson that stopped that lunatic from killing you the first time we met.'

'Quite right,' said Shaw. 'A debt which can never be repaid in this mortal life.'

'Och,' muttered McPherson and looked away, but Shaw could tell the man was gratified.

'And you've been mixed up in some more nasty business I hear,' said Ludd.

'Oh yes…?' replied Shaw cautiously.

'Up in McPherson's part of the world,' said Ludd.

'The papers said it was a massacre.'

'One ought not to believe everything one reads in the newspapers, Chief Inspector,' said the clergyman. 'Perhaps I shall tell you about it some time.'

'Perhaps,' grunted Ludd. 'Seems you've solved almost as many murder cases as I have.'

'Will you be needing me?' asked Shaw.

'Where were you when the…event…occurred?' asked Ludd.

'Just here,' said Shaw, indicating the small table at the foot of the stage. 'I was the prompter.'

'I'd appreciate you staying on then, sir,' said Ludd. 'I'll want to talk to anyone who was within a few feet of the stage.'

Shaw nodded his assent. The hall had now fallen quiet as the last of the stragglers left; the two elderly ladies at the ticket table were politely dismissed by Ludd.

Madame Dubois then appeared from behind the curtains; Shaw noticed she was a striking figure in her theatrical costume, and her stage makeup emphasised her dark features. Ludd and McPherson instinctively stood to attention and clasped their hat-brims.

'I assume you are detectives?' she asked. 'May we please go home? Mrs Hexham is quite obviously dead and there is nothing more anybody can do. It is clearly distressing for her husband.'

'Not just yet, madam,' said Ludd. 'I'll need to speak to everyone who was close to the stage. I haven't even had a proper look at the lie of the land yet. Can we get these curtains opened?,' he called out to nobody in particular.

As if on cue, the curtains opened, revealing the full tableau of horror to the detectives. Nurse James had placed a coat over Mrs Hexham's body; the torn and bloodstained curtain lay nearby.

Ludd bent down and lifted the coat, regarding the corpse quizzically for a few moments.

The cast and various backstage helpers were huddled downstage and in the wings, all scrupulously keeping the corpse out of their gaze but regarding the newcomers with interest. Shaw waved briefly to his wife, who regarded him with a relieved expression.

PC Arbon pushed his way through the crowd and briefly saluted the detectives.

'Arbon, sir,' he said proudly. 'Village constable, just appointed. I've taken names and addresses and also taken a suspect in charge.' He pointed to Havering, who was still slumped in a chair at the side of the stage.

'What charge?' asked Ludd.

'Well…er…I don't rightly know, sir,' said Arbon. 'He ran off after the, the incident occurred, and I caught him making off over the fields. He wouldn't stop when I called, neither.'

'Hmm,' mused Ludd. 'Have you arrested him then?'

'Well…not exactly, sir…' said Arbon.

Ludd sighed. 'All right; McPherson, go and stand by him and just see he doesn't try to leave. If he does, arrest him for fleeing the scene of an accident or something. I'll speak to him first.'

McPherson left the stage and stood between Havering's chair and the exit door at the side of the stage.

Hexham pushed his way through the gaggle of onlookers and confronted Ludd.

'That's my wife lying there,' he said, pointing at the corpse and quivering with anger. 'Are you just going to stand around as if she's invisible or are you going to let me have her taken away to lie decently in our front room?'

'I'm sorry sir,' said Ludd slowly, 'but it's my duty to ascertain just what happened here this evening. We'll be as quick as we can and I'll make sure your wife will be treated with the utmost decorum. That's why I'd like to clear the stage as soon as possible.'

Hexham seemed placated, and returned to his place in the wings.

'Do we all have to stay here?' called out a man's voice from the opposite side of the stage. 'Some of us have homes to go to.'

'Yes, yes all right,' said Ludd. 'I only want those who actually saw what happened on stage. Anyone who was backstage or whatnot can go home, as long as you've given your name and address to the constables.'

There was a murmur of conversation and the majority of the supporting cast and technical crew drifted away. Nurse James stepped forward.

'Will you need me?' she asked. 'I only volunteered to assist the…victim…because there was no doctor in the house. I'm a nurse, you see. And there's a lady backstage who I ought to take home and put to bed – Mrs Bardell, the director. She fainted when she heard about the…accident.'

Ludd touched the brim of his hat. 'I see, madam. Yes, you can go.'

Nurse James hurried backstage and Mrs Bardell's plaintive voice could be heard fading away as the pair left by the back door. 'Simply awful, my dear. Awful…it reminds me of the Zeppelin raid on the Gaiety Theatre when I was playing there, with dear…oh what was his name now…?'

Ludd sighed and turned to PC Tanner. 'I'm guessing you're on late turn at the police house,' he said. Tanner nodded. 'Off you go then,' said the Chief Inspector, 'and when you get there, telephone to Midchester and ask them to send the police doctor and the photographer. Oh, and the duty undertaker as well. Look sharp about it.'

Tanner fumbled a salute and hurried out through the front door of the stage. Ludd then turned to Arbon. 'And you're off duty by the looks of it. You can clear off home too.'

'I don't mind staying, sir,' protested Arbon. 'After all it was me what apprehended the suspect.'

'We'll manage quite well, thank you,' said Ludd. 'And there's no "suspect" and nobody's been "apprehended", so don't get carried away. We'll call for you at the police house if you're needed.'

'He ain't going nowhere without me,' said a pretty young woman with an elaborate blonde hairstyle, who had been waiting in the wings. She wore a modern raincoat over her Elizabethan costume, and seized Arbon by the arm.

Arbon looked sheepishly at Ludd. 'My, er, sweetheart sir. Iris, I mean, er, Miss Garrod.'

'How do,' said Ludd with a brief nod in the woman's direction. 'Make sure he gets home safely, won't you?'

The woman sniffed. 'He's a hero, is my Fred. Went after that murderer without a thought for his own safety, he did.' She clutched her paramour closely, and Arbon's face flushed red.

'What makes you say "murderer"?' asked Ludd. 'Far as we know this is just a nasty accident.'

'Accident! Not likely,' said Iris disdainfully, as she led Arbon down the steps at the front of the stage. 'I'm surprised nobody done her in sooner. And I don't care who hears that, neither.' She cast a glance at Hexham.

'Now just a moment, Miss....' said Ludd, but Iris and Arbon had already left the hall.

'People have murder on the brain these days,' muttered Ludd to himself. He blamed the cinema, and those cheap yellow-backed novels that seemed to be everywhere now.

'Who on earth would be daft enough to murder someone in front of fifty people?' said Ludd to nobody in particular. He then took a deep breath and crossed the stage to where Shaw was standing.

'Before I start questioning people,' he said in a low voice, 'I'd like a word with you first, Mr Shaw. It would be helpful if I could get a sort of summary from a trusted observer; a point of reference if you like from which to judge the other accounts.'

'Very well,' said Shaw. 'Might Mrs Shaw be permitted to stay? I believe she was in the wings assisting with costume changes, and will have viewed things from a slightly different perspective.'

'Right-o,' said Ludd. 'Everyone kindly go into the backstage room, except Reverend and Mrs Shaw,' he ordered the remainder of the cast and crew. 'I'll call you up on stage as I need you.'

There was low murmuring from the audience as they made their way off through the wings to the backstage area. Havering, still on the chair at the side of the stage, stood up to join the others.

'Not him,' commanded Ludd, and McPherson's large hand pushed the young man gently back down on to the chair. Havering sighed, and stared into space once more.

After sending the remaining cast and stage crew into the rooms behind the stage, Ludd called to McPherson again. 'Keep that gent further backstage,' he said. 'I don't want him hearing anything up here and I don't want him talking to any of the others.'

McPherson replied with a nod, and escorted Havering away from the stage.

Ludd then turned to Shaw and his wife. 'Now then Mr Shaw,' he said, 'I'll deal with you first. Just let me know as concisely as possible what you saw occur at the time of the...accident.'

Shaw paused for a moment, trying to recollect the incident.

'Hamlet, that is, Mr Havering, went to stab Polonius, played by Mr Weekes, who was standing behind the curtain.'

'What curtain?' asked Ludd.

'This one,' said Shaw, indicating the heap of white cloth, stained with blood, which lay on the floor next to Mrs Hexham's body. 'It was pulled down by Mrs Hexham as she fell.'

'I see,' said Ludd. 'And what was Mrs Hexham doing behind there, when it was supposed to be Mr Poloni...I mean, Mr Weekes behind there?'

'She was there to assist with the spreading of theatrical blood over the curtain and Mr Weekes' costume, to give the appearance that he had been stabbed,' replied Shaw.

'But for some reason, she copped it instead,' mused Ludd. 'I don't suppose she said anything? No last words that might be of any use?'

'Come to think of it,' said Shaw, 'I do believe her lips moved as she lay on the floor. But I did not hear her speak.'

'I think I may have heard,' said Mrs Shaw. 'I was a little closer. There was a sort of horrible moment of silence just after she fell, and she said something. It sounded rather like...well I can't quite be sure.'

'Have a try, madam,' said Ludd, encouragingly.

'Well, it was something like "you later", or perhaps "you hate her". I honestly am not sure.'

Ludd frowned. 'Never mind Mrs Shaw. If she did say something, one of the others on the stage must have heard. I'll concentrate on what we know for certain for now.'

He pointed down at the floor to where a bloodstained dagger was lying. 'This is the weapon, I assume?'

Seeing Shaw's nod, he crouched down and, using his handkerchief, carefully lifted the knife from the floor and held it to the light.

'Looks like a nasty bit of work,' said Ludd, with a note of irritation in his voice. 'Why on earth was this being used? Don't they use wooden swords and daggers in the theatre, or even india-rubber nowadays? It's not surprising somebody got killed if this was being thrust into people.'

'That is what I do not understand,' said Shaw. 'Prior to the performance a technical rehearsal of this particular scene was held, in which it was shown that the dagger was harmless, with a blunt and retractable blade.'

Ludd gingerly touched the tip of the blade and then, holding the end of the dagger's handle, pressed it into the floorboards of the stage.

'There's nothing retractable about that,' he said.

'Then that must mean that at some point...' began Shaw.

'...a substitution occurred,' added Ludd. 'I see we are thinking along the same lines, Mr Shaw. But where's the dummy?' He walked upstage and called behind the scenery. 'Does anyone know the whereabouts of the retracting knife?'

There was much murmuring and sounds of movement from behind the stage. 'I see it,' cried Madame Dubois finally, as she mounted the stage from the wings. 'Look, by the curtain.'

Ludd stooped down and, using his handkerchief, picked up another knife which looked remarkably similar to the one that Havering had dropped on stage. But there was a difference; he gingerly prodded the end of the knife and it moved half an inch or so into the handle.

'Thank you madam,' he said to Madame Dubois. 'Go

back stage again if you would, please.'

After she had left, Ludd inspected the dagger again. 'This one's the dummy all right,' he said. 'Though what it's doing on stage as well is anybody's guess.'

Shaw thought for a moment. 'Clearly there has been some confusion over the real and dummy knives. What is not clear is whether it was deliberate or accidental.'

'Come along now, Mr Shaw,' said Ludd with a sigh. 'Sometimes your view of human nature is a little too optimistic. What's the likelihood of a real knife that looks exactly like the dummy one being left lying around so's the leading man could pick it up by mistake? '

'But that's simply horrible!' exclaimed Mrs Shaw, who up until this time had remained silent. 'Why on earth would somebody do such a thing deliberately?'

'Well, my dear,' said Shaw, 'We perhaps ought to tell the Chief Inspector about the letters.'

'Letters?' asked Ludd.

'Oh dear, yes, I suppose we ought to,' said Mrs Shaw sadly.

'You see, Chief Inspector,' explained Shaw, 'Mrs Hexham was not a well-liked person. She is rumoured to have been in the habit of sending what I believe are called "poison pen letters".'

'You know me well enough to know I don't deal in rumours,' said Ludd with a frown. 'I leave that to the newspapers. Do you have any evidence of this allegation?'

'Not…exactly,' said Shaw, 'but I did happen to overhear two members of the theatrical group discussing one such letter. The contents sounded really rather distressing and unpleasant.'

'Enough to make someone want to murder the writer?' asked Ludd.

'Perhaps,' said Shaw. 'The recipient, or at least, her

husband, sounded particularly angry and announced that he was going to do something about it.'

'Hmm, better than nothing, I suppose,' said Ludd, 'but it's not hard evidence until I see it. Who was it you overheard?'

'*Must* I tell you, Chief Inspector?' said Shaw sadly. 'I feel I am betraying a confidence.'

'Don't be silly, Lucian,' said Mrs Shaw. 'There is no "confidence" to betray. They were speaking in the open air next to a public thoroughfare and they ought to have realised they might be overheard.'

Shaw noticed the Chief Inspector suppress a grin at the admonitory tone of Mrs Shaw's voice, and looked expectantly at the cleric.

'Well, sir...?' he asked.

'It was Mr and Mrs Cranston, who run the local post office,' said Shaw reluctantly.

'And did either of them make specific threats?' asked Ludd.

'Not...as such,' said Shaw. 'Cranston said he was going to confront Mrs Hexham, and that he would take action if she did not stop sending such letters.'

'Hang on, were these letters signed?' asked Ludd.

'No,' replied Mrs Shaw 'but from what we have heard they must have been from Mrs Hexham. It was clear they were from someone who was concerned about being dismissed from the theatrical committee, which would only mean her.'

'And Mr Cranston said he recognised the handwriting also,' added Shaw.

'Hmm' replied Ludd. 'When Cranston said he was going to take action, he didn't happen to say anything like "I'm going to arrange for that young chap to stab her to death on stage," I suppose?

'Nothing of the kind,' said Shaw.

Ludd sighed. 'I didn't think it would be that easy. Right then. Mrs Shaw, did *you* see anything?'

'Not really,' said Mrs Shaw. 'I was standing in the wings – stage right – no, that's the other side, Chief Inspector, it's the other way round in the theatre, you see – yes that's it – and I only saw what my husband saw, albeit from a slightly different angle. I shouldn't really have been there, because Mrs Bardell, our director, doesn't like people watching from the wings. But it was such a dramatic scene, that I was very keen to see it. '

'I see,' replied Ludd. 'So it was only Havering, Mrs Hexham and this chap Weekes on stage, with you in the wings?' asked Ludd.

'No,' replied Mrs Shaw. 'Mr Cranston was opposite me, in the wings, stage left. He was there to ensure the curtain, the one that they were hiding behind, was pulled back at the end of the scene. There was Madame as well of course. Madame Dubois, playing Hamlet's mother.'

'Madame?' asked Ludd with a raised eyebrow. 'French, is she?'

'Belgian.'

'Ah. And where was she?'

'On the long chair,' said Mrs Shaw, indicating the rather tatty property centre stage.

Ludd walked to the couch and sat on it, looking in the direction of the heaped curtain on the floor.

'Well, she must have seen it all as well,' he said. 'Havering stabs through the curtain, gets Mrs Hexham, she falls down, pulls the curtain, and then Havering runs off, through…through those doors there?'

Ludd pointed to the exit doors at the side of the hall.

'Correct, Chief Inspector,' replied Shaw. 'Constable Arbon, who was off duty, gave chase and whilst doing so, charged me and Special Constable Tanner with keeping the audience in the hall.'

'You both did a good job of that,' said Ludd, 'but then again they're a well-behaved bunch round here. I wouldn't have fancied your chances in keeping the second house locked in at the Midchester Regal.'

'Do you think it might…might be deliberate?' asked Mrs Shaw tentatively. 'After all, why would Mr Havering run off like that if it were some terrible accident?'

Ludd seemed lost in thought, then looked up. 'Did Havering get a poison pen letter?'

'Not as far as I know,' said Shaw. 'The only one I have heard specific reference to is that sent to the Cranstons.'

Ludd was about to speak but was interrupted by the sound of the front doors of the hall opening. A dishevelled looking man carrying a camera was accompanied by a ponderous, bowler-hatted man carrying a gladstone bag.

'Ah, here's the doctor and photographer,' said Ludd. 'You can run along now, Mr Shaw, and Mrs Shaw,' he said genially, 'but thank you for the information. I fancy McPherson and myself have a long night ahead of us speaking to Havering and the other witnesses, but we'll get to the bottom of this.'

Shaw collected his hat and coat from the chair on which he had been sitting, and paused before leaving the hall.

'Ought some announcement be made about Mrs Hexham?' he asked. 'The villagers are no doubt going to be talking about things, and we would do well to quash any rumours before they spread too far. When the audience was sent home they had not even been informed of Mrs Hexham's death.'

'I'd forgotten about that,' said Ludd. 'Comes of working too long in a big place like Midchester where people don't know each other so well. Thank you for the reminder.

Perhaps you would be good enough to tell anyone who asks, including any so-called gentlemen of the press, that Mrs Hexham is sadly deceased and a police investigation is underway into the possible causes. Let's leave it at that for now.'

'No mention of murder?' asked Shaw.

Ludd frowned and raised his hand. 'Let's not be too hasty, Mr Shaw. For now I'm not airing any theories in public. Let's just say between friends, however, that I think something's rotten in the state of Denmark, as the saying goes.'

'How apt to quote from the play, Chief Inspector,' said Shaw. 'You are familiar with the text of *Hamlet*?'

Ludd looked at Shaw with a puzzled expression. 'Never seen it in my life before,' he replied.

Mr and Mrs Shaw were about to leave but Ludd suddenly called out. 'Wait, Mr Shaw!'

The clergyman turned to look at the detective quizzically.

'If it's not too much to ask, sir,' said Ludd, 'on second thoughts perhaps you'd stay on. I wonder if you might be a bit of reassurance for the witnesses, so to speak, when I'm talking to them. After all it's a nasty business and people are bound to feel a bit shaken up.'

'Of course,' said Shaw. 'I wanted to remain for that very reason, but did not wish to intrude on your investigation.'

'I think I know you well enough by now to not worry about that,' said Ludd. 'Take Mrs Shaw home, won't you, and then once you're back we can get started.'

'I tell you I had no idea it was a real bloody knife!' insisted Havering, as he jumped up from his chair. He was the first to be spoken to by Ludd and McPherson in the small room at the back of the hall, while Shaw stood by as pastoral observer.

'Watch your language when there's a minister about,' said McPherson gruffly, pushing the young man back into his seat. Havering seemed to have lost his earlier taciturnity and was now freely speaking on the events of the evening.

'I can't see why *he* needs to be here anyway,' said Havering, looking suspiciously at Shaw.

'He's here to provide moral support to his flock, on my request,' said Ludd. 'And that's an end of it. Now, you say the dagger was always kept in the belt of your costume, is that right?'

'Yes,' said Havering, then rapidly added 'but only when I was wearing it, of course.'

'What do you mean by that?' asked Ludd.

'I mean, I had the dummy knife on stage during the technical rehearsal,' said Havering, 'even the vicar saw that.'

Shaw nodded, and the young man continued. 'But I wasn't in costume then, so I put the knife in the properties cupboard behind the stage. Hexham – he's sort of the stage manager – doesn't like things like that to be left lying around in case they go missing.'

'Stolen, you mean?' asked Ludd.

'No,' corrected Havering. 'People leave things in the wrong place and so on, and just when you need a property – props we call them – you find they've been left somewhere else, so we always made sure anything like that was put in the cupboard.'

'Locked, is it, this cupboard?' asked McPherson.

'No,' said Havering sullenly. 'Anyone could get into it if they wanted to. I went back home after the technical for a quick supper, and somebody could have substituted the knife then.'

'Well that's possible I suppose,' said Ludd as he took the two weapons from the brown envelope in which he had placed them earlier, and positioned them side by side on the little folding card table at which he and Havering sat. Using his own handkerchief, Ludd lifted each knife in turn, assessing their weight and testing the mechanism of the knife with the collapsible blade.

'Hard to tell until we get these dusted for prints,' he said, 'but I accept they do feel a little similar, at least in weight. And they look similar.'

'Bert Cranston, I believe,' interjected Shaw, 'made the weapons from the same type of kitchen knife, so it is likely they will feel similar. But do you not notice there is a difference?'

Ludd stared at the knives, and attempted to push his hat brim up, presumably to remove the shade from his eyes; the felt merely buckled at the touch of his knuckles.

Ludd's eyes flicked upward. 'Blasted soft thing,' he muttered, and then he looked back down at the knives.

'Jewels,' said McPherson, looking intently at the daggers. 'The dummy one's got some sort of imitation rubies stuck on the hilt, the other has'nae. Just circles o' red paint.'

'I was about to say that,' said Ludd, tetchily.

'Of course,' said Shaw. 'I noticed the gleam of the jewelled handle during the technical rehearsal, but not during the actual performance.'

'Look at the difference,' said Ludd, pointing to the hilts of the two daggers. 'The working knife looks much the same but those jewels are just painted on, pretty crudely as well. Surely you would have noticed that, Havering?'

The young man sighed. 'It's almost pitch black behind that stage and I was in a rush to get ready, I just took the knife out of the cupboard without giving it a second glance.'

'So how do you explain,' queried Ludd, 'the fact that the dummy knife was found on the stage near the curtain? Somebody must have brought that on stage from the properties cupboard. Was that you?'

'Why on earth would I bring two knives on stage?' said Havering. 'I tell you, I only brought one with me, and that was the one from the props cupboard.'

'All right, all right, said Ludd. 'But you must have realised something was wrong when you stabbed the knife through the curtain?' asked Ludd.

'Of course I damned well did!' snapped Havering. 'In the technical rehearsal the blade just went smoothly into the handle of the knife when it hit Weekes. I knew straight away something was wrong when the blade met so much resistance, as if it had gone into...I think I'm going to be sick'.

McPherson, standing behind Havering's chair, placed his hands on the young man's shoulders but Ludd made a waving gesture.

'Let him go, McPherson,' he said with a sigh.

Havering rushed to the small wash-basin in the corner of the room and vomited noisily for a few moments.

After he returned and sat down, Ludd pushed a packet of Players' Weights across the table to him.

'Take one, you look done in,' he said.

With a trembling hand, Havering pushed back a strand of hair from his forehead and extracted a cigarette from the packet and put it in his mouth. Ludd lit it for him and the young man sighed with relief as some colour returned to his face.

'I knew right away something was wrong,' he said calmly, 'and when Mrs Hexham fell forward, I realised there had been a terrible accident. I couldn't take it in, and I suppose that's why I bolted.'

'Poor show if you ask me,' said McPherson. 'Could you no' have stayed to help, instead of running off like that?'

'You're both too young to have fought in the war,' said Ludd. 'Men can do odd things after a shock like that. Mr Shaw can vouch for that, I should think.'

'Indeed,' said Shaw. He suspected Ludd was attempting a more friendly approach with Havering, and decided to assist. 'I have unfortunately had to counsel one man who killed one of his comrades by mistake in the heat of battle,' he added.

'Quite,' said Ludd. 'So we can understand why you made a run for it. What I would like to know is, did you hear Mrs Hexham say anything after she fell?'

'Come to think of it, I did,' said Havering. 'It was just a whisper really. 'I'm pretty sure what it was though. It was "you traitor"'.

'Definitely that?' asked Ludd. 'Not "you hate her", or "you later"?'

'No, it was definitely "traitor"', replied Havering. He took a long drag on his cigarette; his old confidence seemed to have returned.

Suddenly Ludd changed tack, and leaned forward towards Havering. 'Ever had any letters from the deceased, son?' he asked bluntly.

'L...letters?' asked Havering. Shaw noticed that beads of perspiration had suddenly appeared on the man's forehead.

'Yes,' said Ludd. 'Poison pen letters. We think Mrs Hexham was sending them. Nasty ones, too. Did you get one?'

Havering was silent, and greedily drew on his cigarette. His eyes darted between Ludd and Shaw.

'We've ways of checking,' said Ludd, 'so you'd better tell me the truth.'

Shaw wondered if Ludd really did have "ways of checking" but the bluff, if it was one, seemed to work.

'All right, yes,' said Havering with a sigh.

'What did she write in them? asked Ludd.

'I...I'd rather not say,' said Havering. 'It was personal.'

'How many letters?' asked Ludd.

'Just one,' said Havering quickly.

'Where is it?' demanded the Chief Inspector.

'I...don't know,' said Havering quickly. 'Honestly I don't.'

'All right then, I'll ask again,' said Ludd. 'What did Mrs Hexham write in her letter to you? A brief summary is all I need. And don't tell me you can't remember.'

'As I said before,' replied Havering, more confidently this time, 'It was personal. I'm not sure if I know where the letter is now anyway, so that's all there is to it. I don't believe you've any right to keep me here without charging me with something. May I go now?'

'We'll tell you when you can go,' growled McPherson.

'All right, sergeant,' snapped Ludd. 'I'm in no mood to play silly games. It's going to be a long night and until you decide to tell us what was in that letter, I'm having you taken in charge.'

'On what charge, exactly?' sneered Havering.

'For refusing to comply with a constable's order to stop, him having reasonable grounds to suspect a crime had been committed,' replied Ludd gruffly. 'Take him over to the police house, McPherson. Oh, and get him out of that ridiculous costume first, or the village will think there's a pageant in progress.'

Chapter Five

'Do you really think there might be more to this than an accident?' asked Shaw, after McPherson had left to escort the young man down the road to the police house.

Ludd rubbed his chin. 'I'm not ruling anything out at this stage,' he said. 'But that callow youth is holding something back – he admitted it himself – and I don't need that sort of obstruction at this stage in the proceedings. A night in the village cells might help change his mind. Besides, I didn't like his tone.'

'He does seem a rather over-confident young man,' mused Shaw.

'Met his sort in the war,' said Ludd with distaste. 'Fresh out of public school and thought they could lord it over men twice their age, just because they had one pip on their cuff.'

Shaw smiled briefly. 'I knew such men also. With most of them it was merely bravado. If it really was an accident, Havering has had quite a shock, and is probably attempting not to show it. The matter will weigh heavily on his conscience.'

'Perhaps you're right,' said Ludd. 'Well let's have a word with the others. Would you be so kind as to fetch Mr Hexham in here? I'd better speak to him next.'

Shaw duly obliged, and Hexham was brought into the

little changing room.

'I've asked the vicar to sit with us, Mr Hexham,' said Ludd, 'as you've no doubt had quite a night of it. I'll be as brief as possible under the circumstances.'

'Thank you,' said Hexham.

He appeared solemn, but composed.

'Where were you when the incident occurred?' asked Ludd.

'Incident?'

'Ah…when your wife was fatally, er, wounded.'

'I was behind the curtain.'

'I thought only Mr Weekes and your wife were there.'

'No, I was there also. I was standing between my wife and Mr Weekes. In fact, just behind them.'

'What were you there for? I understand your wife was intending to throw some sort of theatrical blood, but surely that didn't need two people?'

'I was there to assist Mr Cranston with the removal of the curtain for the next scene. It's quite a heavy bit of cloth and needed two people to do it, one at each end.'

'Where was Mr Cranston?' asked Ludd.

'He was waiting in the wings,' replied Hexham. 'He was there to help me with the curtain.'

'Couldn't you just have come on from the, er, wings to do that?' enquired the Chief Inspector.

'Not really enough time,' said Hexham. 'Mrs Bardell – that's the director – wanted quick scene changes, just the lights going off and on again. So I needed to be behind the curtain ready to move as soon as possible. It's a tight squeeze and dark back there, and there'd be an awful lot of bumping about if Mr Cranston and I tried to get on at the same time.'

'Could Mr Cranston see what was going on behind the curtain?' asked Ludd.

'Not from where he was standing, I would have thought. No, definitely not,' said Hexham.

Ludd was silent for a moment, then fixed Hexham with a steady gaze from across the little card table.

'I realise this is a difficult question, but did *you* see your wife being stabbed? The actual blade, coming through the curtain?'

'No, thank God,' replied Hexham in a neutral, flat tone. 'I knew something was wrong though, as she froze after the line when Hamlet was supposed to stab her...what was it now...?'

'"Dead for a ducat, dead",' prompted Shaw.

'That's right,' replied Hexham. 'Thank you, vicar. She was supposed to throw the theatrical blood over the curtain, and over Weekes' costume at that line, but she just stood still. I stepped forward between her and Weekes to see what was wrong, but then she fell forward and pulled the curtain down. And then she was...'

His voice broke and Ludd raised a hand. 'All right, Mr Hexham. Thank you. You didn't happen to hear your wife say anything, at any time during the...unfortunate occurrence?'

'No,' said Hexham, his tone now one of curiosity. '*Did* she say anything?'

'We're not sure,' said Ludd briskly. 'Thank you sir, that will be all,' he added, standing up from the table to indicate that the interview was over.

'What about my wife's...body?' he asked.

'I'd like the police doctor to have a look, if you don't mind, sir,' said Ludd gently. 'Just to make sure we have all the facts necessary for an inquest.'

'Inquest?' asked Hexham.

'Yes,' replied Shaw. 'Coroner's inquest. Always happens in a case like this. We just need to get to the bottom of what happened.'

'But it was deliberate, surely anyone can see that,' said Hexham.

'We don't know that yet sir,' said Ludd carefully, 'but I hope to find out exactly what *did* happen, and *why*. I'll arrange for your wife's body to be moved to a suitable place for you in due course. I expect Mr Shaw here will be able to arrange the, ah, necessary duties.'

'That's a weight off my mind,' said Hexham, looking at Shaw with a wan smile. 'Thank you as well, Chief Inspector. I'll be getting home now. It's been a rather trying day.'

'Very good, sir,' said Ludd. 'I may need to call on you again in the next few days, but for now, get some rest, eh?'

Hexham smiled wanly again and left the room slowly, stoop-shouldered, holding a handkerchief to his mouth.

'Poor basket,' said Ludd, shaking his head. 'He's holding it all together but I doubt he'll keep it up for long. You'll keep an eye on him for me, Mr Shaw?'

'Of course,' said Shaw. 'As you mentioned, I will need to discuss funeral arrangements with him. I note you did not mention the matter of the poison pen letters.'

'Well spotted Mr Shaw,' said Ludd. 'He's had enough of a shock seeing his wife drop dead in front of him. I don't think he's ready to find out she was up to no good at her writing desk. I'll have to break that to him gently next time I see him. Now who else do I need to speak to? There's Weekes, who was behind the curtain, and Madame, what's her name…?'

'Dubois,' said Shaw.

'Dubois,' echoed Ludd with an exaggerated French pronounciation. 'She wasn't much closer than you were to the action, if she was on that settee in the centre of the stage, so I'll see her last.'

'Last?' asked Shaw. 'What of Mr and Mrs Cranston, or indeed the rest of the cast and helpers? Anyone could have substituted that knife in the properties cupboard. One of two dozen people, perhaps.'

Ludd pushed his hat back and rubbed his eyes, then looked at his wrist-watch.

'Mr Shaw,' he said with a sigh, 'that's just it. It *could* have been anyone who substituted that knife. It may not have even *been* substituted; we've only Havering's word for that. So let's not get carried away. It's gone eleven o'clock and there isn't time to interview everyone in the whole village, so I need to concentrate on the most important witnesses tonight. That's why I sent the rest home.'

'Of course,' said Shaw apologetically. 'Shall I fetch Mr Weekes?'

'That would be very kind,' said Ludd.

A few moments later Shaw showed Weekes into the changing room. The man, now changed into his normal clothing, was visibly shaken, but primly declined the offer of a cigarette from Ludd.

'Never touch them,' he said primly. 'Asthma, you see. Weak chest.'

'Very well, Mr Weekes,' said Ludd. 'I'll be as brief as possible. I'm trying to get an idea of exactly what happened on the stage tonight. We'll come to motives later. Just tell me what you saw when Mrs Hexham was stabbed.'

Weekes paused, took a handkerchief from his top pocket and dabbed his forehead. Shaw caught a whiff of some sort of cologne – lavender, he thought – from the article. Weekes swallowed, and then spoke hurriedly, as if he wanted to get the information across as quickly as possible.

'I was standing next to her...Mrs Hexham, that is,' he said, 'and just as she was supposed to throw the blood over the curtain and my costume, she fell forward and pulled the curtain down. Then she was dead on the stage in front of me. That was all I saw.'

'You didn't see her actually being stabbed?' asked Ludd.

Weekes paused and swallowed again. 'No,' he replied eventually. 'It was dark, I could hardly see anything.'

'And did you hear Mrs Hexham say anything, either before she was stabbed, or afterwards?'

There was another long pause.

'Try to think, please, Mr Weekes,' insisted Ludd. 'It could be important.'

'Yes,' replied Weekes eventually, his eyes darting between the Chief Inspector and Shaw. 'I think she said something like "I hate her" but I can't be certain.'

'Not, "traitor"? asked Ludd.

'It might have been,' said Weekes. 'I really wasn't thinking properly. It was all so...'

The man began to slump forward and Shaw steadied him.

'I think I'd like to go home,' said Weekes. 'It's all been rather trying.'

'Of course, sir,' said Ludd. 'Just one more thing. Did you receive any letters recently from the deceased?'

There was a pause, and Shaw noticed Weekes' adam's apple working up and down.

'Letters?' he asked lightly.

'Yes,' said Ludd. 'Letters making...accusations, perhaps.'

'Accusations?' replied Weekes quickly, with a note of anger in his voice. 'Why on earth should she do that? No, no, I didn't get any letters from her.'

'All right sir,' said Ludd. 'That's quite in order. You may

go now. Thank you. Oh, but before you go, would you ask Madame Dubois to step in?'

Weekes merely nodded, and left the room quickly, as if glad to escape.

'Shifty,' said Ludd to himself, then he looked up and remembered that Shaw was in the room.

'What was that, Chief Inspector?' asked the cleric.

'Nothing, just thinking aloud,' said Ludd wearily. 'After I've spoken to this lady, with any luck McPherson will have finished tucking up Havering at the police house and we can all get home.'

'Here she is now,' said Shaw, as Madame Dubois entered the room.

'You wish to see me, Inspector?' she said. Shaw, already standing, noticed that Ludd instinctively rose to his feet at her entrance, but then caught himself and sat back down. Madame Dubois had changed out of her costume into a tailored tweed suit of expensive material and highly flattering cut, an outfit which was finished off by a discreet felt hat with a small feather in it, and a fur stole around her neck.

She sat primly at the table, and brusquely declined Ludd's offer of a cigarette after examining the brand name on the packet.

'It's Chief Inspector,' said Ludd. Madame Dubois did not reply, but merely looked at him with an expression of slight boredom.

'Bit of a long way from home, aren't you?' asked Ludd.

'I live just outside the village,' replied Madame Dubois. 'What do you mean?'

'I mean, a long way from Belgium,' replied Ludd.

'And so?' she said with an arched eyebrow. 'England is my home for many years now.'

'What part of Belgium are you from?' enquired the Chief

Inspector genially.

'Liège,' she replied curtly. 'I don't think you will know it.'

'*Au contraire*, as they say,' replied Ludd. 'I was in a depot there for a few weeks after the war, just after we kicked Jerry out. Hell of a mess to clean up.'

Madame Dubois appeared uninterested in Ludd's attempts at polite conversation. She turned to Shaw.

'Why is the priest here?' she asked.

'Mr Shaw has kindly consented to be present as a pastoral advisor. Everyone's had a nasty shock tonight and I thought a bit of moral support would be useful.'

'I understand,' said Madame Dubois. 'I however have no need of this "moral support". Unlike you I spent much more than three weeks in Liège and it was under German occupation, not British. I have seen far worse things than the death of that…that woman.'

Madame Dubois almost spat the last two words, and Ludd raised an eyebrow.

'If you could just tell me what you saw when the incident behind the curtain occurred, madam,' said Ludd.

'I saw very little,' replied Madame Dubois. 'Ronnie – I mean, Mr Havering, stabbed into the curtain, and then she fell down and was dead, so.'

'Must have been a bit of a shock,' said Ludd.

'Yes, but only because I did not think someone would do that in front of so many witnesses.'

'What do you mean by that?'

'I mean that woman was a bad person, and I am only surprised it took so long for someone to kill her.'

'No love lost between you then?'

'*Comment?*'

'I mean, you didn't get on with Mrs Hexham.'

'Nobody liked her, except…except her husband, for

some reason...I just feel sorry for Mr Havering to have killed her in such as way that his guilt was there for all to see.'

'You mean, you think Havering stabbed Mrs Hexham deliberately?'

'Mais bien sur! Of course, why else would he have done it?'

'Havering says it was an accident. That somebody substituted the dummy knife for a real one.'

Madame Dubois uttered a short laugh and moved her shoulders in a way that Shaw thought was probably what was known as a 'gallic shrug.'

'It sounds insane,' she said. 'It was a, how you say, crime of passion. He was angry with Mrs Hexham, he stabbed her, and *eh voila*, she is dead. Perhaps he did not mean to kill, but only to hurt her. I do not know.'

'Why are you so sure it wasn't an accident?' enquired Ludd.

'Because that *salle*...that old woman was sending letters of, how are they called, the black mail, to people. I received one and so did Mr Havering.'

'I see,' said Ludd, with a hint of satisfaction in his voice. 'Now we're getting somewhere. Did anyone else receive a letter?'

'Ophelia – Mrs Cransonne – Mr Havering, and myself.'

'You're sure that's all? How do you know?'

'We talked of the matter this evening while getting ready for the play. We were all angry about it.'

'Have you any idea what was in Mr Havering's letter?'

'I do not know. None of us discussed the contents, only that they were of the black mail, and that she needed to be stopped.'

'Stopped, as in killed?'

'Pfft, I mean removed from the theatre company,' said

Madame Dubois with a wave of her gloved hand. She leaned forward conspiratorially.

'But my suspicion is,' she continued in a low voice, 'that whatever was in Mr Havering's letter, it was bad enough to make him *fou* – mad with rage, and to use a real knife with which to kill Mrs Hexham.'

'In front of all those witnesses?' asked Ludd incredulously.

'As I say, he must have been mad,' replied Madame Dubois. 'All that mattered was his revenge. He perhaps did not think in the straight way.'

'Hmm, perhaps,' said Ludd, rubbing his chin. 'And what was in *your* letter?' he asked.

Madame Dubois paused, her face flushing with colour. 'I do not wish to say,' she replied.

'Something bad enough to make you want to kill Mrs Hexham as well?' said Ludd.

Madame Dubois slammed a gloved fist on the table, making Ludd flinch. 'I am not some mad woman, Chief Inspector, who flies into a rage because some evil witch writes me a filthy letter! I have, how is it called, self control. I am not stupid enough to risk the executioner simply to silence that, that, old devil!'

There was a tap on the door and McPherson's head appeared around it.

'Havering's all dealt with sir,' he said.

'Very good,' replied Ludd. 'Doctor and photographer finished?'

'Aye sir, they're just off the now. The deceased's being taken to the Midchester mortuary.'

'Right then. Who locks the place up, Mr Shaw?'

'I believe the caretaker is Mr Samson, in the cottage over the way.'

'Thanks,' replied Ludd. 'Look him up, McPherson, and

tell him we'll be out of his way in a few minutes but he's to keep the place locked up until further notice.'

McPherson nodded, and his head disappeared behind the door.

'But what of the two more performances over the next days?' asked Madame Dubois incredulously. 'There is the English saying is there not, "the show must go on"?'

'Not when a murder might just have been committed,' said Ludd wearily. 'We'll be back in the village tomorrow first thing, and we'll doubtless be spending a lot of time here over the next few days. I'm not having a bunch of actors prancing about in here while I'm looking for evidence.'

'A fuss over nothing,' said Madame Dubois, shaking her head. 'I wish to go home, I am tired,' she added.

'All right, all right madam,' said Ludd gently. 'Just one more question and then I shall let you go. Did Mrs Hexham say anything before she died? I mean, when she collapsed on the stage?'

Madame Dubois looked puzzled. 'No, I do not think so,' she said. 'I did not hear anything. Why?'

'Just checking,' said Ludd. 'We think she might have said the word "traitor". That mean anything to you?'

'It means nothing to me.'

'Very well,' said Ludd, rising from his chair. 'Thank you very much for your co-operation, Madam; that will be all for now.'

Madame Dubois smiled and offered her hand to Shaw and then the Chief Inspector, who appeared slightly flustered and shook it rather too hard, as he would a man's hand.

'"Traitor" was her last word, you say?' asked the Belgian, pausing at the doorway of the changing room.

'That's what we think, anyway,' said Ludd.

'Strange,' replied Madame Dubois. 'It is definitely of no meaning to me.'

Half an hour later, Ludd's motor car was humming along the main road from Lower Addenham to Midchester, its headlights creating only a short tunnel of light ahead on the road; all else was smothered in the inky darkness of a Suffolk winter's night.

'Are you sure it was a good idea to have that minister sitting in on those interviews, sir?' asked McPherson, whose drooping eyelids betrayed the fact that he was fighting sleep. 'I saw you even gave him your home telephone number. He's no' going to go blabbing to the papers or anything is he?'

'Don't be daft,' said Ludd, who felt fully awake, his mind churning and sifting the information he had gleaned in the course of the evening's work. 'You only met him on that murder case two years ago. Don't forget I was with him during that business over at Eastburgh* as well.'

'Aye, I was on my holidays then.'

'And didn't I know it. I was short-handed and I don't mind saying I was baffled – absolutely baffled by that case but it was Shaw that worked it all out. I've a feeling our job in Lower Addenham will be much easier if we've got him on our side this time as well.'

'If you say so sir,' replied McPherson, 'but if the Chief Constable gets wind of it…'

'The Chief Constable needn't know. And he'd better not find out because if he thinks we can't clear something like

---

*See The Wooden Witness

this up ourselves he'll have Scotland Yard down here before you can say Jack Robinson. He'll do anything for a quiet life on the golf course, that one.'

A few moments later Ludd slowed the car down to enter the narrow street of terraced houses in Midchester in which McPherson and his new wife had lodgings. McPherson looked at his watch and cursed.

'Late back again,' he muttered.

'Mrs McPherson's not nagging you about that yet is she?' asked Ludd with a chuckle. 'You've only been married five minutes.'

'No,' said McPherson wearily. 'It's the landlady. Gives me a ticking off if I come back late. Says it lowers the tone o' the household.'

Ludd barked a laugh and looked out at the frost-rimed, mean little houses with their grimy net-curtained windows and soot-stained walls, marked with the chalk-scribbles of children. Someone, an adult, presumably, judging by the height from the ground at which it had been written, had chalked 'JESUS DIED FOR YOU' in large letters on the brick wall of a small factory; beneath it someone else had scrawled an obscene rejoinder.

The street was dimly illuminated by two flickering gas-lamps at each end. He saw a figure with a ladder approach the lamp-standard and realised it was the lamp man; it was midnight and the time for the lights to be turned off.

After the man had made an adjustment to the lamps, the street was plunged into darkness, the only light coming from the icy quadrant of the moon, low in the sky.

The street looked more squalid and miserable than ever in the cold lunar light, and Ludd suddenly felt a pang of pity for his sergeant. As McPherson reached out to open the passenger door, Ludd stayed his arm.

'Just a minute,' he said. 'How much are you paying for that flat?'

'Six and a tanner,' said McPherson. 'Why?'

'Six shillings and sixpence a week? For a couple of poky rooms in that place?' asked Ludd incredulously. 'Board included?'

McPherson laughed bitterly. 'No chance. Jean has to buy her messages – the shopping, I mean – herself.'

Ludd made a snap decision. 'Listen here. Why don't you come and lodge with us for a while. Just until...well, give you a chance to save up a bit of money. Some of the new villas round our way are on these payment plans, mortgages, they call them, forty pounds down and then you pay off the rest in stages. Put your mind to it and you could save that up in a year.'

'I don't know about that, sir...' said McPherson doubtfully. 'I'd feel obliged to pay rent to you.'

'So you'd have to,' chuckled Ludd. 'I'm not offering charity my lad. How about five bob a week and board included, for the back bedroom at our house? That's big enough for you to make a sort of bed-sitting room out of it. I wouldn't expect you and the wife to sit with us in the front parlour of an evening and sing hymns round the piano, if that's what you're worried about.'

'It's tempting,' said McPherson, rubbing his chin. 'I'll have to talk it over with Jean.'

'You do that,' said Ludd, pushing open the passenger door of the car. 'No hurry. I haven't mentioned it to Mrs Ludd either, but I think she'll like the idea. She and your wife got on like a house on fire at your wedding. I think she reminds her of our eldest girl.'

'Aye, they did get on well,' said McPherson. 'Will your daughters no' want the room, though?'

Ludd chuckled. 'Those two? Not likely. Too busy living

the high life in Ipswich and Norwich. There's always the small spare room if one of them wants to visit.'

'I'll let you know then, sir,' replied McPherson. 'And thanks.'

'No trouble,' said Ludd genially. 'Get some sleep, we've got a long day tomorrow back at Lower Addenham. And don't let that landlady push you around.'

McPherson stepped out of the car and crossed to the door of his lodgings; Ludd pulled away from the kerb, chuckling at the idea of the burly Scots policeman being subjected to a tongue-lashing from some dragon of a landlady with her hair in curlers.

'Six and six a week,' he muttered, as the car picked up speed a few moments later on the Midchester bypass. 'Disgraceful.'

The village of Lower Addenham, a little larger than most villages, but not quite large enough to be considered a market town, had some fifteen hundred or so inhabitants. The news of the shocking event at the village hall had spread quickly amongst nearly all of them that evening, transmitted vocally over pints of bitter in the George, garden fences, and the walls of adjoining privies.

'Have you 'eard?' became the watchword of the night, as worried villagers cautiously bolted their doors and locked their windows. 'There's bin another one' was another common refrain; the village having known murder only a couple of years previously; then that had been followed by another killing* in a country house a few miles away.

*See The King is Dead

The reaction of the village to the previous events had been one of shock mingled with excitement; the death of Mrs Hexham was, by contrast, regarded with grim resignation. Such things were now 'the way of the world' or 'the way things were going'; some villagers saw it as simply another signpost on the long road to perdition that had become the inevitable destination of the entire country.

It would not be long, some said, before the village high street resembled Chicago, with gangsters firing tommy guns at each other from speeding motor cars.

It was universally believed that Mrs Hexham had been murdered – 'she had it coming to her' – was the verdict in the court of public opinion held in the George tavern that night. Ronald Havering seemed the obvious suspect, especially as he had been taken by a plain-clothes man to the village police house.

One particularly fervent drinker in the George, a devotee of Hollywood drama, declared that something called a 'lynch mob' should be got up to deal with Havering before he could do any more harm, but he retreated sulkily to the privacy of the snug following laughter and shouts of 'this ain't the Wild West you silly beggar,' from his fellow tap-room lawyers.

By the next morning, the gentlemen of the press had been alerted and a small gaggle of reporters dogged Shaw as he made his way from the vicarage to Morning Prayer in the nearby parish church. The verger barred them from entering, urging them to 'have a bit o' blasted respect' and using other terms not generally heard in the east doorways of country churches.

Following his devotions Shaw gave a brief statement in the churchyard to the reporters, who went away somewhat disappointed that the death of Mrs Hexham had not officially been declared a murder, and that Havering was only being held on a minor charge.

Shaw was therefore slightly irritated when, half an hour or so later, he was interrupted in his study whilst working on his sermon.

'Beg pardon sir,' said Hettie, the maid-of-all-work as she responded to her master's call of 'enter', 'but there's a…young person to see you.'

'A young person of the journalistic variety, I assume?' asked Shaw wearily.

'No sir,' said Hettie, with a note of considerable curiosity in her voice. 'It's Gladys. I mean, Miss Kersey. Says it's a personal matter.'

'Very well,' said Shaw, wondering what on earth the barmaid of the George might need to discuss with him. He always paid cash there, so there could not be any account that he had overlooked. 'Show her in please.'

Then as an afterthought, he added 'by the way, Hettie, I see that my other surplice has not yet been ironed. Would you be so kind as to have that ready for me to take over to the vestry this morning?'

He wondered if Hettie would guess this was largely a ruse to ensure she would be in the kitchen at the far end of the house, and thus unable to accidentally eavesdrop.

If she did, it did not show in her face, and after she had shown Gladys in, he heard the domestic trudging down the corridor to the kitchen.

'Good morning, Miss Kersey,' said Shaw, as he rose from his desk. 'Won't you sit down?'

'I'll stand thank you vicar,' she replied tersely.

'May I offer you some tea?' enquired the clergyman.

'No thanks,' said Gladys. 'I don't mean this as to be a social call.'

Shaw looked at her. She might have been a textbook example of the radiant natural beauty of young English womanhood, had that not been spoiled, in Shaw's eyes, by the artificiality of waved hair and inexpertly applied cosmetics, topped by a cheaply made and gaudily patterned hat and coat.

'How may I be of assistance?' asked Shaw genially, relighting his pipe and adding to the thin blue haze of smoke in his study.

'It's…well I don't rightly know where to start,' she said.

'The beginning is generally the best place,' said Shaw.

Gladys took a deep breath. 'It's about Ronnie. Mr Havering, I mean to say.'

'I see. What of him?'

'After what happened last night, well most of us, that is, from the village hall, went over to the George. Well, we needed a stiffener, you see.'

'A…stiffener?'

'A strong drink. After the shock of what happened, like.'

'I see.'

'And…well, you know how word gets around in this place.'

'Indeed I do.' Shaw puffed silently on his pipe for a few moments, allowing Gladys to continue. She took another deep breath.

'The long and short of it, vicar, is they're saying it was Ro...Mr Havering done it by accident. That they're going to let him off. '

'I believe the police have not yet come to any particular conclusions,' replied Shaw.

'Be that as it may,' said Gladys primly, 'but I say as it weren't no accident.'

'That is a rather serious accusation, Miss Kersey. On what do you base this assertion?'

'I've...well to put it plainly vicar, I know I've done wrong. I daresay I might even go to prison over it, as I've heard some do. But I was up all night thinking about it and I thought to myself it's my dooty to speak up.'

'Are you sure this is not a matter for the police?' asked Shaw cautiously. 'Chief Inspector Ludd...'

'I saw him at the hall last night,' said Gladys quickly, 'and that other one, the Scotsman. Didn't like the look of either of them, and I didn't want to talk to them about it. It's personal, like. I saw you was helping them when they was asking questions, and I thought I'd rather come to you about it and then you can pass it on, like.'

'That is kind of you to have confidence in me,' said Shaw, 'but you do realise you may still be required to discuss the matter with the police?'

'Be that as it may, I'd rather it come through you first. Then they'll see as I'm making an effort to...to live decent, like.'

'Forgive me Miss Kersey, you will have to speak more plainly if I am to be of assistance. Just what is it you wish to say in regards to the case?'

Gladys squeezed the cheap artificial snakeskin handbag that she held in front of her, and continued.

'Mr Havering and me, well, we was courting for a while. Sweethearts, like. But then...'

Oh dear, thought Shaw. He guessed what all too common revelation was to come next.

'But then,' repeated Gladys, 'I found I was expecting. I know I done wrong, but well, he said he loved me and I thought he was going to propose to me any day.'

Shaw sighed. 'And no such proposal came?'

'No,' replied Gladys sadly. 'I told him what had happened, and that we'd have to be wed, all proper-like, in church. But he said no. And what was worse, he laughed at me. Yes, laughed. Said did I really think the likes of him would marry the likes of me? And he said that it was my own fault for...for what had happened. Said I led him astray.'

Shaw could not help wondering at how predictable the Tempter was in his assaults on humanity. It was a story, he reflected, as old as Adam and Eve.

'Then he says to me,' continued Gladys, 'as he would sort it out. He knew a doctor who would fix me up.'

Shaw swallowed hard. His next question was to have been when she was due, so that the necessary arrangements might me made. He felt his heart sink.

'You are saying that Havering procured a...'

'I won't give it a name,' said Gladys quickly, 'but yes, he made all the arrangements.'

Shaw sighed. 'Why did you not come to me earlier?' he asked. 'There are organisations, societies to whom I could have referred you. Mrs Shaw used to work for one such. There was no need to...'

'You don't understand, vicar,' said Gladys sadly, shaking her head. 'Me dad would have found out, and that would have been that. I'd lose me job and I'd be on the streets.'

'But all that may well happen now anyway,' said Shaw. 'And in addition, you may have to serve a prison term.'

'Judging me and all now, are you?' asked Gladys coldly.

Shaw tapped his pipe out on the little Benares brass ashtray on his desk, and stood up, placing a hand on Gladys' shoulder.

'It is not for me to judge you or anyone. I am perfectly willing to treat everything you have told me in absolute confidence if you so wish. But if this has some bearing on the killing of Mrs Hexham, I will be honour bound to speak to Chief Inspector Ludd about it.'

'I know that,' said Gladys sadly, 'and I'm willing to take the consequences. He can't be allowed to get away with what he done.'

'You mean,' replied Shaw, 'for arranging the…'

'I don't mean that,' said Gladys quickly. 'All right, he might have said I had to do it, and paid for it, but in the end it was down to me as much as him. No, I'm not talking about that. I'm talking about what he done to Mrs Hexham.'

'Are you sure you won't sit down?' said Shaw, returning to the seat at his desk. Gladys merely shook her head.

'I didn't have anyone to talk to about it, not with mother gone,' she said. 'So I talked to Mrs Hexham about it. I know some as didn't like her, but she never gave me no trouble. One day during rehearsals, just after I'd…had the thing done…I was feeling poorly and had to rest, and she came in the back room to see if I was all right and then, well, it all came out. I told her everything.'

'And she confronted Havering?' asked Shaw.

'Not so far as I know,' said Gladys with a sniff, 'but she said she would make sure he suffered for what he done. I begged her not to, but she said he was a cad and a rotter and would have to pay. So she must have talked to him about it. And I reckon that's why he killed her.'

'But why?' enquired Shaw. 'Why go to such lengths?'

'You don't know him, vicar,' said Gladys. 'He's charming all right but he's also a brute, especially when he's been drinking. Got a nasty temper on him. My thinking is, Mrs Hexham must have told him he had to leave the group and he wouldn't stand for it.'

'And you think he was willing to kill her over that?' asked Shaw incredulously.

'I don't know,' added Gladys, 'but I reckon she might have, you know, threatened him. Said she would tell what he made me do. He could go to prison for that and all, couldn't he?'

Shaw was uncertain about the law on this particular topic, but he had read of such cases, where several parties including the mother to be, father and facilitating doctor had all been prosecuted. He nodded.

'So I reckon,' said Gladys, 'he tried to stop her by stabbing her, and then blamed it all on having the wrong knife. There,' continued Gladys, dabbing at her eyes with a handkerchief. 'I feel better now it's all come out. Calm, sort of. You'll tell the police?'

'I believe it is my duty,' said Shaw.

'All right then,' said Gladys, as she pushed the handkerchief up her sleeve and composed herself.

'I do not think I will be able to keep your name out of the matter,' said Shaw, 'but I will endeavour to put in a good word on your character to the police, and to mention that you may have been coerced.'

'Very well, vicar,' said Gladys gravely, and turned to go. 'Do you think there's...forgiveness, for what I done?'

'I do not wish to give you a religious lecture,' said Shaw, as he rose from his chair, 'as I suspect you have suffered enough. Be sure however that there is *always* forgiveness for those who truly repent.'

'I...I'll try, vicar,' said Gladys warily.

'You are still very young,' said Shaw, 'and you have your whole life ahead of you. If this is made public you may however be better off moving to some place where you are not known.'

'I know that vicar,' said Gladys, and tried to smile. 'I've a mind to move to London when this is all over. I'd wanted to for a while anyway.'

'Please let me know your address and I shall write to the parish priest asking him to visit you.'

'You don't need to bother.'

'Very well, but one word of advice as your clergyman. In earlier days you would have been uncharitably considered a "fallen woman." Such a description is rarely heard nowadays, fortunately. You may still have a chance of finding a good husband; a decent man of similar background to your own. Promise me therefore you will stay away from the likes of Ronald Havering.'

Gladys hesitated, then whispered 'I promise. And thank you.'

She stood on tiptoe and kissed him on his cheek as if he were some kindly uncle, and before he could ring for Hettie to show her out, she was gone.

Chapter Six

After Shaw had prayed for guidance in his study, he put on his hat and coat and left the vicarage. He recalled that Chief Inspector Ludd had said he would be back in the village early in the morning, and so his first port of call was the police house to enquire of his whereabouts.

'Morning vicar,' said PC Arbon genially at the desk of the tiny reception room in the police house, which amounted to little more than a large brick-built cottage with a blue lamp outside the front door. 'Rum old do last night, weren't it?' he said. 'I've already had to tell a couple of reporters outside to bug…to buzz orf. What can I do for you?'

Upon learning that Shaw was looking for Chief Inspector Ludd, he lifted a little flap in the desk and beckoned for Shaw to come through.

'You've come to the right place,' said Arbon. 'His nibs is just talking with the prisoner while he's having his breakfast. I've done the fingerprinting,' he said proudly. He then looked shamefaced at the inkstains on his hands and attempted to rub them off on his trousers. 'Blasted messy job,' he said under his breath.

There was the sound of a metal door closing and Shaw saw Ludd and McPherson emerge from a little cell built into the corner of the room. Ludd frowned.

'Ah, Mr Shaw,' said Ludd. 'I know we asked you to help out but I didn't expect you to be on parade first thing in the morning.'

'I came as soon as I could, Chief Inspector,' said Ludd. 'Matters have arisen pertaining to the case which I think you should know about. May we speak in private?'

'Matters, Mr Shaw?' said Ludd. 'Sounds ominous. This your parlour back here, constable?' he asked, pointing to a door at the rear of the office.

'That's right sir,' said Arbon, going to the door. 'It's a bit untidy mind...perhaps if I just cleared up a bit...'

'No need,' said Ludd. 'You stay here with McPherson and get Havering's paperwork finished off, give him his personal items back and so on. Then you can let him go.'

'Ah, if I may, I suggest you do not let Mr Havering go just yet,' cautioned Shaw.

'Oh yes?' said Ludd with a raised eyebrow. 'I think these "matters" you're about to tell me might be rather serious. Come along then. Keep Havering here for the time time being, constable.'

Arbon looked puzzled, but hurried away with a 'very good sir.'

They entered the little low-ceilinged parlour, where Arbon's long combinations were drying by the fire. A litter of sporting papers and magazines covered the sofa, and the remains of the policeman's breakfast was on the table. Shaw told Ludd all he had heard that morning from Gladys Kersey, with the exception of mentioning the young lady's name.

Ludd pushed his hat back on his head and lit a cigarette, gazing into the little fire meditatively. He inhaled smoke deeply, then burned back to Shaw.

'And this young woman is willing to give evidence?' asked Ludd.

'I believe so,' replied Shaw. 'Although if possible I think her name should be kept out of it.'

'I can't guarantee that,' said Ludd. 'In fact it's highly unlikely. Still think she'll testify?'

'Most definitely. She did not have to reveal any of this, she only did so out of concern that Havering killed Mrs Hexham.'

'We've only got her word for that,' said Ludd. 'What if she just wants revenge on him for knocking her up and then refusing to marry her? What's the old saying? "hell hath no fury like a woman scorned".

'*Hamlet* again...' murmured Shaw.

'What's that?'

'Nothing. I think it highly unlikely she would risk a prison term and the entire loss of her reputation merely for petty vengeance.'

'Hmm. She could well go to gaol for what she did, it's true.' Ludd took a last drag on his cigarette and threw the stub in the fire. He then punched his right fist into his open palm.

'It's a risk but I'll take it,' he said. 'Havering's from a wealthy family, he could do a bunk to the continent tonight and we might never see him again. I can't risk that happening. If we can't get him on murder, we'll have him on that other thing. That sounds more serious than just some backstreet old crone doling out hot baths and gin.'

Shaw winced with distaste but Ludd was oblivious, and carried on talking.

'I know some Scotland Yard chaps are building a case about a doctor – a Harley Street surgeon, if you please – who's involved in that business. They might be very interested to hear about this. Yes, I think it's worth a shot. Come along then.'

When the two men re-entered the police office, they

were greeted with the sight of Havering lounging in a wooden chair, having a cigarette lit for him by Arbon. McPherson was absorbed in filling in an official form at the desk.

'Morning vicar, morning Chief Super, or whatever your name is,' chirped Havering. 'I must say I don't think much of the breakfast in this establishment. All I got was porridge.'

'You might have to get used to that,' said Ludd sternly.

'Eh?' asked Havering.

'Stand up please,' said Ludd sternly, 'and put that cigarette out.'

Havering shrugged and stood up, then tossed the cigarette end on the linoleum floor and stood on it.

'Ronald Charles Havering,' intoned Ludd, 'I am arresting you on suspicion of murder contrary to common law, and for the procurement of an abortion contrary to the Offences Against the Person Act 1861.'

Havering stared open mouthed. 'What the…'

'That's enough from you,' snapped Ludd. 'McPherson, lock him up again will you. He can stay here for now.'

Amid shouted assertions of his father's high standing with the chief constable of the county, Havering was bundled unceremoniously by Arbon and McPherson back into the little cell.

'Is that it then, sir?' asked Arbon, breathing heavily as he and McPherson returned from the cell. 'Case closed, as they say?'

'For the time being,' said Ludd.

'The time being?' asked McPherson. 'Did he kill her or not? I'm a wee bit confused.'

'Step outside for a moment, would you, sergeant, and Mr Shaw too,' said Ludd. 'Getting a bit crowded in here. I'm sure you've got something to be getting on with, constable. You can clean up those living quarters for a start.' Arbon blushed and disappeared into the little parlour behind the front room.

'That's better,' said Ludd as they stepped outside. 'Don't want the likes of PC Arbon listening in and giving his two ha'porth.'

The air outside the police house was beautifully fresh compared to the stale fug inside; Shaw breathed in deeply and noted the sunlight dappling the woods and fields just beyond the edge of the village. He loved this kind of day; of neither winter nor spring but something in-between that seemed unique to this particular part of England.

His reverie was broken by a flash of white in the corner of his vision. Ludd was using his handkerchief to flick some dust off the windscreen of his car, which was parked on the grass verge next to the police house.

'Can't seem to keep her clean,' he muttered.

'Yours, Chief Inspector?' asked Shaw. 'It does not appear to be a police car.'

'That's right,' said Ludd. 'Just got her. Transformed my working day, that has. Means I can get to the station or to places like this to get on with the job much faster. It beats the station pool car hands down. I think in years to come every copper will have to have his own motor car.'

'We must indeed count our blessings,' said Shaw. 'I fear it will never come to pass however that every clergyman has his own motor car. Where will you drive to next?'

'At this moment,' said Ludd, putting his handkerchief away in his breast pocket, 'I think I shall walk. I'm going to speak to Mr and Mrs Cranston at the post office. It's only up the road.'

'I still don't understand, sir,' said McPherson, who was finishing his first cigarette of the day nearby. 'If Havering did it, what are you speaking to the Cranstons for?'

Ludd relayed to McPherson what Shaw had told him about the recent developments in the case. McPherson nodded.

'The business with the young girl sounds like a dead cert. Should be no trouble building a case,' he said. 'But the murder? Have we got enough for that? Do you not think it's like Havering said, just a terrible accident?'

'Not after what Mr Shaw told me,' said Ludd. 'I think Havering knew what he was doing all right with that knife. He thinks we're daft enough to believe his story about not feeling the difference between the real dagger and the dummy one. We'll see about that when the fingerprint boys have finished with them. We've got no rush. He's not going anywhere for a while as with that other charge hanging over him he'll be put on remand.

'Now off you go round to his house. If they won't let you in, we'll get a search warrant. I want that letter from Mrs Hexham found. If it's got something juicy in it it's more evidence that he knifed her deliberately. It's that big old place just off the Midchester road, only a few minutes walk. Wait for me here when you've finished. '

'Right sir,' said McPherson, and hurried off down the lane away from the village.

'Perhaps you'll walk with me Mr Shaw,' said Ludd. 'Or do you have...whatever it is you clergymen do all day...to do this morning?'

Shaw smiled. 'I will walk with you part of the way, as I wish to call on Mr Hexham.'

'Oh yes?' said Ludd, as they walked slowly along the village high street. 'Got any theories?'

'Theories?' replied Shaw. 'No, no, this is a pastoral visit. The man is in mourning. There are funeral arrangements and so on to be discussed.'

'Of course,' said Ludd. 'Once the police doctor's finished

with her. On that topic I had a telephone call earlier this morning and he says the body will be released in a couple of days. Taking a bit longer than usual, but I know he's overworked so I didn't say anything. I'll let you know.'

'Thank you Chief Inspector,' said Shaw. 'On a different, but similar topic, I do have something of a "theory" I should like to air.'

'And what might that be?' said Ludd.

Before Shaw could answer, a little baby Austin screeched to a halt in front of them. A weasel-faced man in a belted raincoat and trilby hat, with a press card stuck in the band, leaped out and raised a metal object; there was a flash of light and Shaw was momentarily blinded by purple spots in front of his eyes.

When his vision cleared he saw the figure lowering a camera and leaning towards him, uncomfortably close. 'Fred Gutteridge, *Midchester Evening News*,' said the man rapidly in a nasal voice. 'Care to make a statement, vicar? The readers want to know if you're going to solve this case before the police, like all your other ones.'

Before Shaw could answer, Ludd stepped forward and pushed the man back with his palm, causing him to stagger backwards on to the bonnet of his tiny car, which made a sound of popping metal in protest.

'Here, leave off you, I'm just asking questions,' said the reporter. 'Take your blooming great paws off me. Who do you think you are anyway?'

Ludd took his warrant card out of his pocket. 'Chief Inspector Ludd,' he said, showing the document to the journalist. 'You nearly ran us down just then and if you bother this gent again I'll have you taken in charge. Clear? Now, hoppit.'

'How do you know about other cases I have been involved with?' asked Shaw irritably. He was mildly angry at the sudden intrusion into the calm of the village morning, but also intrigued.

'Our newspaper archive,' said Gutteridge proudly. 'We can find out anything there. Here, have my card if you want to talk.'

He managed to shove a grubby business card into Shaw's top pocket before Ludd bundled him back into his car. 'Clear off,' said Ludd, 'before I tip this kiddie-car over with you in it.'

'Blasted reporters,' continued Ludd as the baby Austin disappeared in a cloud of blue exhaust fumes. 'They've all got cars or motor-bicycles nowadays and appear like a load of vultures when you least expect it.' He adjusted his hat and coat and the two men resumed their walk along the lower end of the village high street.

McPherson had no difficulty finding Kenilworth Lodge, Havering's rambling family home; he did, however, have some difficulty gaining entry. He at first had to leap back as a baby Austin motor car shot past him on the drive, tootling its horn and filling the detective's trouser-turnups with a spray of gravel.

As he walked up the little carriage-turn he shook his head in disbelief at how the other half lived. This old Tudor house with its various wings and extensions could contain at least a dozen flats of the size he and his new wife were living in.

Immediately after he had rung the old-fashioned bell-pull in the little gabled porch, the heavy studded door flew open and a red-headed maid rushed at him with a besom.

'I've already told you, you can clear off, the pair of yous! The master's not speaking to any reporters – didn't your mate in his motor car just now tell you that? You're the tird one this mornin'!'

'Look you, I'm no' a reporter,' said McPherson gruffly. 'And put that broom down,' he added, looking at the bristles which were positioned perilously close to his nose, 'or I'll break the thing in half and beat your backside with it.'

'And who the devil are you if you're not a reporter?' asked the maid suspiciously, lowering the broom slightly.

McPherson sighed and raised his warrant card. 'I'm a police officer. Is Mr Havering senior at home?'

'What's this about?' demanded a stern voice from inside the house. A man in late middle age with a fine head of grey hair and an aristocratic bearing, wearing ancient but well-cut tweeds, appeared behind the Irish maid.

'Mr Havering?' asked McPherson. 'Detective Sergeant McPherson. Can I talk to you in private?'

'Go inside Maeve,' said the man in a tone that indicated he was used to giving orders. 'Madam wants you in the kitchen.'

'Very good sir,' said the maid, glowering at McPherson as she disappeared into the house.

'I was just about to telephone the local constable,' said Mr Havering. 'I hear my son's got himself into a spot of bother. '

'A wee bit more than that, sir,' said McPherson. 'May I come in?'

Mr Havering showed McPherson in to a small book-lined study off the main hall of the house.

'That hack that came round earlier was spouting a lot of nonsense about my son stabbing some woman in the village hall,' said Mr Havering. 'It's obviously all a lot of nonsense or some sort of rag – he was in trouble for that sort of thing at Oxford, I recall once I…'

'It's no a "rag" as you call it sir,' interrupted McPherson. 'He's being held on suspicion of murder.'

'Held, where?'

'The village police house, for the time being.'

'I don't believe it.'

Mr Havering slumped into a leather armchair.

'He'd been out all night of course,' he continued, 'but he often does that, young chap like that in the prime of life. Wild oats and all that. I was the same at his age. I've warned him about it of course, but what more can one do? It's bound to be a mistake. Look here, I must go and see him. I have friends you know, Sir John Ellison, the KC, for a start. He'll…'

'We'll come to that in a moment sir,' said McPherson, raising his hand. 'Before that I'd like to have a look round his room.'

'Certainly not,' said Mr Havering angrily. 'Unless you've got a warrant.'

'I've no warrant,' said McPherson, 'but in a case like this I can easily get one. It'll help your son if I can have a look through his things as soon as possible. It might turn up something that'll help in his defence.'

McPherson suspected it was more likely that he would find something that would help in his prosecution, but he knew that mentioning it would not assist him in gaining entry.

'Very well,' breathed Mr Havering. 'Suspicion of murder, you say?,' he added in disbelief.

'Aye, and there's another charge too,' said McPherson.

A few moments later an ashen-faced Mr Havering had summoned Maeve to show McPherson to his son's room, on the strict understanding that he was not to discuss either of the charges with the servant or Mrs Havering, whom he had told in no uncertain terms to remain in the kitchen.

McPherson methodically searched the bedroom, rummaging through drawers and a wardrobe bulging with well-cut suits bearing the labels of various Savile Row tailors.

He finally located a pile of letters in the bedside cabinet, most of them tailors' and tobacconists' bills, with a few *billet-doux* from women with very good addresses in London; he then frowned with distaste as he found a small packet of pharmaceutical items hidden inside a copy of *La Vie Parisienne*. Returning them to the cabinet he scanned the pile of letters again, then his heart raced as he found more than what he had hoped for.

'It's a sad business, Mr Shaw,' said Hexham as he showed the vicar into the small study at the front of 'The Old Lodge', the solid, double-fronted Queen Anne house off the village high street. The widower was wearing a black suit of old-fashioned cut, which lent him an almost elegant air.

'Care for some tea?' he said. 'The daily left a pot. Might still be warm.'

'Ah, no thank you, Mr Hexham,' said Shaw. 'I will not take up too much of your time, as I am sure you have plenty to do. I merely came to see how you are getting on.'

'Quite so, quite so,' said Hexham, clearing a pile of paperwork away from an armchair. 'Won't you sit down?'

Shaw sat on the armchair and Hexham placed himself at the bureau in the corner.

'Yes,' he continued. 'Lots to do. Our two boys are both in the colonies – Kenya and Uganda – I daresay they won't be able to return for a few months, but I'll have to write. Then there's all the various legal papers and the funeral to arrange.'

'On that topic, perhaps I may be of some help?' asked Shaw.

'I don't think so, vicar,' said Hexham briskly. 'My wife didn't hold with your church. She was Baptist, you see.'

'I did hear that,' said Shaw, 'but I understood she was no longer in communion with that denomination.'

'She was treated rather badly by the minister,' said Hexham, 'so I shall be writing to a Baptist clergyman of my acquaintance in Midchester who I hope will carry out the service at the civic cemetery.'

'Very well,' said Shaw. 'If I can be of any further assistance, please do not hesitate to ask.'

'Thank you,' replied Hexham. He paused for a moment then spoke again. 'There is one thing.'

'Yes?'

'Am I right in understanding you know the investigating detective, Chief Inspector Ludd, quite well?'

'Our paths have crossed on one or two occasions. Why?'

'Well, you can tell him from me, that I think he's done the right thing. Arresting Havering.'

'May I ask why?'

'In case you're wondering, vicar, I know about the letters. The ones my wife sent.'

'Ah.'

'I know she was a…difficult person. But she meant well.

She had high standards and expected those that worked with her to have them as well, myself included, and if they fell short, well, she put them in their place about it.'

Shaw did not quite know how to respond to this, so he merely nodded.

'Havering made it clear he didn't like my wife. He wanted her out of the troupe, you see. If you ask me it was because he's lazy and didn't like being told to turn up on time and so on. Mrs Hexham was a stickler for punctuality. He and the others were planning to vote her off the committee, you know. That's why she sent the letters, the letter I mean, to Havering. Giving him a last chance to drop the idea.'

'Have you any idea what was in this letter?' asked Shaw.

'No, but my wife wasn't one to mince words. She would have told him in no uncertain terms to reconsider his position.'

'I see. Forgive me Mr Hexham, I know this must be difficult, but do you really believe this would make Mr Havering wish to kill your wife? And in front of so many witnesses?'

'He's a nasty piece of work,' said Hexham. 'Turned up tight once or twice to rehearsals as well. Bad-mouthed my wife, as well. Of course he did it.'

'He claims it was an accident.'

'He can claim what he likes. The law won't fall for that, though.'

'Were any other letters sent by your wife? To other members of the group?' asked Shaw cautiously.

There was an awkward silence.

'There…might have been,' said Hexham finally. 'I didn't discuss it in great detail. But as I say, Jean, that is, Mrs Hexham, is…was…a stickler for correct behaviour and she may well have had occasion to upbraid some of the other group members from time to time. It's possible she wrote other letters asking the committee to reconsider voting her off. That group was the only social activity she had, apart from the Wednesday knitting circle at the village hall.'

'In that case, surely there could be other suspects?' asked Shaw. 'Other members of the group who wished harm to your wife?'

'There may well have been – nobody likes being told they are in the wrong, Mr Shaw, and my wife was not one to hold back if she saw wrong-doing – but let us not forget it was Havering who stabbed my wife, in full view of everyone! Any speculation on others being involved seems pointless.'

Shaw realised he was close to overstepping the mark, and that he was intruding too much on a bereaved man. He stood up.

'I shall leave you in peace, Mr Hexham,' said Shaw. 'I shall of course be praying for you. Do call, or telephone to the vicarage if you require any assistance at all.'

'That's very good of you,' murmured Hexham as he raised himself from the bureau. As he did so, a pile of papers tipped on to the floor at Shaw's feet.

'Allow me,' said Shaw, and bent down to pick the papers up. As he handed them back to Hexham, he could not help noticing it was a title deed for The Old Lodge, Lower Addenham, Suffolk, in the name of Jean Hexham.

Hexham frowned and then showed Shaw to the door. 'She was one of the old school, vicar,' he said. 'A strong woman. Always had the last word. We won't see her like again.'

At the other end of the high street, Ludd was standing in the low-beamed little store room behind the post-office counter of the village stores. It was very different to the gleaming new shops in the parade on the Midchester bypass which he occasionally visited with his wife.

The Chief Inspector inhaled, breathing in a smell which brought back memories of his boyhood – a mixture of boiled sweets, pipe tobacco, cider, fresh newsprint and something else he could not quite identify – something chemical, like paint or turpentine. It was one of those shops that sold anything and everything, including, as he was about to find out, the type of knife that had killed Mrs Hexham.

'I thought we'd gone through all this last night,' said Cranston defensively. 'You've got the man that done it, now what more is there to be said?'

'There's still a few loose ends to be tied up,' said Ludd. 'Is your wife about?'

'She's upstairs in bed,' said Cranston. 'Proper laid her low, did last night. She lived for that group, and to see all that work gone west, well, I doubt she'll be up again for a week.'

The shop's doorbell clanged and Cranston looked out through the store-room door.

''Scuse me,' he said. 'I'm short handed today.'

'No trouble,' said Ludd.

While Cranston attended to the customer, Ludd examined the contents of the store-room. He noticed a newly opened box which contained a number of smaller boxes, each showing a picture of a kitchen knife with the words 'Excelsior, Sheffield' printed above it.

After Cranston returned, Ludd removed his hat and perched on a storage crate.

'I know this is difficult sir, but may I see a copy of the

letter that you received, allegedly from Mrs Hexham?'

'Who told you about that?' growled Cranston.

'Never you mind,' said Ludd firmly. 'I'd like to see it.'

A few moments later Ludd was looking at the dense scrawl of a poison pen letter. He winced at the nastiness of it, one sentence in particular:

> You are not able to have children anymore, are you? Well that is a shame. And your husband, as I am sure you know, is not legally allowed to run a post office. If 'somebody' was to tell the authorities, you would not even have a roof over your head.

'I burnt the first two,' said Cranston. 'Though they were much the same as that.'

'What's this about running a post office?' asked Ludd.

'The old hag must have dug up something in the papers from years ago,' said Cranston angrily. 'I was up on a charge of drunk and disorderly, up Lowestoft way.'

'What happened?' enquired Ludd.

'Knocked a copper's helmet off. Got fined five bob.'

Ludd suppressed a smile. 'Why would somebody blackmail you over that?'

'Cos she was that sort of person, wasn't she?' said Cranston angrily. 'Just wanted her own way all the time and bullied anyone who stood in her way. Reckon she thought the Post Office would sack me if they knew I had a conviction. I never told them about it when we got this place, see. Paid my dues I reckon, and joined that bloody silly Band of Hope, too. Haven't touched a drop since. You don't reckon they'll find out, do you?'

'It's a bit below my pay grade,' said Ludd, 'but I can't see them doing anything as it would look bad on them for not having checked. But what about these remarks to your wife? About not being able to have children?'

'That's all there is to it,' said Cranston bitterly. 'We lost the one last year – vicar will vouch for that as he buried her – and the doctors – two of them, we saw, to make sure, said she can't have any more.'

'That must have made you pretty angry, for someone to write a letter to your wife alluding to it,' said Ludd carefully.

'I didn't kill Mrs Hexham, if that's what you mean,' replied Cranston, slamming his fist down into a cardboard box on the shelf next to him. 'I just wanted it out with her, and for Audrey's sake I was going to keep quiet until after the play was over. But it doesn't matter now, does it?'

'No, I suppose it doesn't,' mused Ludd. He pointed to the box of carving knives he had noticed earlier.

'This the one you used to make the stage knife with?'

'That's right,' said Cranston warily. 'You can buy that knife in every Woolworth's in the country. Why?'

'Care to show me how you did it?'

Cranston carefully removed a knife from one of the boxes. He pointed to the wooden handle.

'I noticed this was quite long, see, compared with the blade. Almost the same length. And, it's made in two pieces. They just comes apart if you unscrew 'em.'

He took a screwdriver from the shelf and worked at two little bolts in the handle; it came apart easily, and he carefully removed the blade and placed it on top of the box.

'I got the idea from a toy I had when I was a nipper,' said Cranston. 'Little metal thing it were, German made I think, it had a knife blade but when you stabbed anything with it, the blade went into the handle on a spring. It looked very realistic. I remember terrifying the girls at school with it, till it got confiscated.'

Ludd could tell Cranston was proud of his handiwork as he continued to explain how he had altered the knife.

'So what I did was, just chiselled out the inside of both halves of the handle and fixed it so's the blade could fit nearly all the way back in, on a little spring, so's it could pop out again. Glued it back together instead of using the screws, as they got in in the way of the blade. Then I dulled the blade on my grinding wheel; well, I thought to myself, it's a sharp one and even if it retracts that could still hurt someone. Then I added a what-do-you-call it, the bit that goes across there?'

'Hilt?' suggested Ludd.

'That's the one. Added that and then a few jewels and things, to make it look old fashioned and sparkle a bit on stage. We sell them here, for the kiddies, like .'

'Can I see them?'

'Used up the last of 'em on that knife. Wholesaler don't make them anymore.'

'All very ingeniously done, anyway,' said Ludd. 'What I want to know is this. Did you ever make a knife with the hilt and jewels and what not, but one where the blade was kept sharp and didn't retract?'

'No,' said Cranston. 'Why would I?'

'Well *somebody* made one,' said Ludd.

'You mean the one that was used to kill Mrs Hexham?'

'Correct. Know anything about that?'

'Course not. Well it could only be one person who made it, surely?'

'And who might that be?'

'The one who used it, of course. Ronnie Havering.'

'And would those two knives – the working one, and the dummy one, feel the same to someone picking them up?'

Cranston appeared puzzled.

'How should I know? I never touched the working one, did I?'

'You've got a whole box of them here,' said Ludd, pointing to the floor.

'I know that,' said Cranston. 'But I haven't got the working one with the hilt and the jewels and that, have I? So I don't know what that one feels like.'

Ludd suddenly cursed himself for a fool. He had forgotten to bring with him a package which he had left in his car; he thanked Cranston and hurried out of the shop to retrieve it.

In a village one often meets acquaintances in the street, often several times in the course of a day, and this day was no exception as Ludd, McPherson and Shaw's paths all happened to converge on the little square beside the war memorial.

'Here's your minister friend again,' said McPherson to his superior, as he noticed Shaw approaching along the high street. 'Listen, do you want me to tell you what I've found while he's about?' he asked doubtfully.

'I'd rather have Shaw where I can see him,' said Ludd. 'he's a useful man to have around but if I don't keep a close eye on him, he'll get himself into trouble again and it'll be us that has to clear up the....ah, Mr Shaw, we meet again.'

The clergyman had now reached the two men in the square, and raised his hat in greeting.

'A fortunate coincidence,' said Shaw, 'as there is something I would like to ask you about the case.'

'Oh yes?' said Ludd guardedly. 'Look here, I was about

to walk back to the police house with the sergeant here. Care to stroll along? Then we can talk on the way.'

'Thank you,' said Shaw.

The three men walked slowly down the hill, only just able to do so three-abreast on the narrow pavement.

'I was prompted by something that Mr Hexham said when I visited him just now to pay my formal condolences,' said Shaw.

'And what was that?' asked Ludd.

'He said his wife always had the last word, which reminded me of her *actual* last word, or words. Which as far as we know were something along the lines of "you traitor."'

'We've been through all this already,' said Ludd.

'Yes,' said Shaw carefully, 'but I have remembered something about when it happened.'

'Pardon us,' said Ludd, raising his hat and sidling awkwardly into the road as a young woman with a perambulator passed them. 'You were saying?'

'I recall that when Mrs Hexham fell, she lay facing with her head pointing stage right. Meaning that when she spoke her final words, she would have been looking in a particular direction at one person.'

'Which was?'

'Madame Dubois. There was nobody else in that part of the stage.'

Ludd pushed his hat back and stopped outside the door of the police house. 'I think you're getting a bit carried away, Mr Shaw,' he said eventually. 'This business of "last words" giving a clue to the identity of the killer is all very well for melodramas, but I can assure you it doesn't happen nearly so much in real life. If they do say anything it usually doesn't mean anything. Look here, you were a padre in the war, weren't you?'

'That is correct.'

'Well then, you must have had to comfort a few dying men, I suppose.'

'Unfortunately that was my duty on several occasions.'

'Ever hear them say anything that made any sense?'

Shaw thought for a moment. 'Not particularly. Most of them, I am sorry to say, called for their mothers.'

Ludd looked down and shook his head, appearing for a moment to be lost in thought. 'Yes, that was what I heard a few times as well. That blasted war. Neither England nor Germany seems any the better for it.'

He looked up. 'Anyway, my point is this, when someone's dying he – or she – doesn't always look you in the eye all lucid like and say something that makes sense. It could just as well be nonsense. Come to think of it we're not even sure Mrs Hexham did say "you traitor", and just because she had her head pointed at this Madame person, doesn't mean she was talking to her.'

'Perhaps…' said Shaw. 'I thought I ought to mention it.'

'That's all right,' said Ludd amiably. 'Seeing as you're here, come inside and we'll let you in on some real detective work. McPherson here's found something interesting it seems, and so have I.'

Chapter Seven

A few moments later Shaw, Ludd and McPherson were seated in the back parlour of the police house holding cups of strong brown tea poured for them out of a large institutional enamel pot by PC Arbon. After telling him to poke the little fire into life, Ludd despatched the constable into the front office to be 'getting on with something'.

'Now then sergeant,' said Ludd. 'What is it you've found out?'

'I searched Havering's room, like you asked,' said McPherson enthusiastically, 'and I found the poison-pen letter.'

'Let's have a look then,' said Ludd.

McPherson took the letter from his pocket, and handed the densely-inked missive to Ludd; he scanned it then handed it to Shaw.

Shaw read it and shook his head; despite having had to confront almost every human sin as part of his vocation, he could never quite get used to the tawdry banality of evil, the almost flippant way with which people misused one another.

He snapped out of his reverie when Ludd asked him a question.

'Unsigned, of course,' said Ludd, 'but it must be from Mrs Hexham. Think that would make Havering worried enough to murder her?'

'It is...possible, I suppose,' said Shaw. 'I do not know the young man, so cannot vouch for his character.'

'His old man said he'd been in trouble for what he called "rags" at university,' said McPherson. 'What does that mean exactly, Mr Shaw? I did'nae want to show myself up by asking at the time.'

'What one might call high-spirited pranks,' said Shaw. 'it was known to happen while I was up – ducking unpopular persons into fountains or sometimes even the Cam itself – and so on. I understand it happens more often nowadays. I have never known it to involve lethal force, however.'

'It might have been some sort of joke gone wrong though,' said Ludd. 'He perhaps just wanted to scare her, give her a bit of a fright and warn her off. He might never have intended to kill her.'

'Aye, I thought about that,' said McPherson. 'But then we can still get him on manslaughter. Either way he'll not be getting away with it. And there's something else I found.'

McPherson took another letter from his pocket and handed it to Ludd, who placed it on his knee and read it while holding his cup and saucer in his hands. He slurped tea noisily, then put the cup and saucer down on the floor.

He passed the letter to Shaw, who quickly scanned it. It was a bill, from a Harley Street surgeon, invoicing Havering ten guineas for an 'examination and surgical procedure.' He frowned as he realised this must be the doctor that had seen Gladys Kersey.

'I'm not entirely sure how the law views that,' said Ludd. 'I know that the young woman will have to be prosecuted. I think that Havering can be as well for abetment. And that letter will be very interesting to the boys at the Yard who are trying to build a case. I'm pretty certain the name on that bill is the doctor they're after. Let me make a telephone call.'

Ludd left the room and McPherson and Shaw sat in rather awkward silence drinking their tea. Fifteen minutes later Ludd reappeared.

'Took a blasted age to connect with London,' he said, 'but at least the chap I wanted to speak to was at his desk. And I was right. That Harley Street fellow *is* the one they want, the dirty beggar. Charging a fortune to "help out" society girls in trouble. Makes you sick, so it does'.

'What was it you were going to tell us, sir?' asked McPherson.

'Oh yes, I clean forgot,' said Ludd. He finished his tea and deposited the cup and saucer on the cluttered table, then took his briefcase from beside the armchair in which he sat. He opened it and took out a brown-paper package.

'Fingerprint boys dusted these last night and got me the results this morning,' he beamed. 'How's that for efficiency? Which is more than I can say for PC Arbon here,' he added as he cleared away the clutter of cups and newspapers from one side of the table. He placed the two theatrical daggers side by side.

'Only one set of prints on them,' he said. 'Bring Havering's set in here, will you, sergeant?'

McPherson fetched the newly-made set of fingerprints from the front desk, and placed it on the table next to a print on a strip of celluloid, lifted from the handles of both knives.

'Perfect match,' said Ludd proudly. 'Nobody's else's on them either.'

'Aye, very good work sir,' said McPherson, 'but it does'nae prove a great deal.'

'All it does prove,' said Shaw tentatively, 'is that

Havering is the only person whom we can say with any certainty has handled both knives.'

'And we know that he did the stabbing anyway, with the real knife, in front of witnesses, so what does it matter?' added McPherson.

'All right, all right you two,' chided Ludd. 'At least let me enjoy for a brief moment the efficient detective work of some of my squad, won't you? And Havering claims someone else swapped the dummy knife for the real one and left it in the props cupboard. No other fingerprints on it makes that impossible to prove. So that's a key part of his defence gone.'

'Aye, it's not looking good, I agree,' said McPherson.

'Is there any significant difference in the feel of the knives?' asked Shaw. 'Could Havering genuinely have mistaken the real one for the dummy?'

'See for yourself,' said Ludd, gesturing to the weapons.

Shaw tentatively picked the two daggers up and handled them.

'The dummy does seem a little lighter, and the blade moves slightly on its spring,' he said.

'Exactly, Mr Shaw,' said Ludd. 'You see it's not so much that they *look* different – the dummy one has jewels but the real one only has the jewels painted on – it's that they *feel* different. Havering might be able to claim he couldn't see the difference in the dark behind the stage, but he would have noticed the difference in feel when he picked the real knife up, surely.'

'Yes, I suppose so, if handling it for more than just an instant,' said Shaw.

'And he must have held it for more than that, because he says he took it out of the properties cupboard and then fitted it into his belt before coming on stage,' continued Ludd. 'Making his claim of it being an accident all rather unlikely. Here's what I think happened.' He leaned forward in his armchair and counted off points on the fingers of his splayed hand.

'Havering gets a blackmail letter. He's the only one who got a letter with something really nasty in it.'

'The Cranstons also received one,' said Shaw.

'Yes, and I read it when I spoke with Bert Cranston earlier,' replied Ludd. 'It was unpleasant and vindictive but I don't think there was anything worth murdering someone for in it. As a blackmail attempt it was feeble – just some petty offence Cranston was had up for years ago.'

'What about the Belgian woman?' said McPherson. 'Did she no' get a letter too?'

'She said she did but she won't show it to us and says it's not important,' said Ludd.

'Should we no be the judge o' that, sir?' said McPherson.

'Yes,' replied Ludd irritably, 'but if I start forcing people to hand over letters or searching through their house without due cause it's not likely to encourage co-operation, is it?'

'Weekes says he didn't get a letter,' continued the Chief Inspector, 'and we've no reason to think otherwise; so the only person who a. could have voted Mrs Hexham off the committee and b. could also be *really* in trouble if she told the authorities what she knew, was Havering.'

'Aye, it does make sense now,' said McPherson.

'Havering got that letter,' continued Ludd, 'from Mrs Hexham, blackmailing him over getting that young barmaid fixed up by a doctor in London. He panicked; he might even have spoken to Mrs Hexham to have it out, and threatened her, perhaps. Issued a counter-threat.'

'A counter-threat?' asked Shaw.

'Yes, you know,' said Ludd. '"You keep that quiet or it

will be the worse for you", sort of thing. Perhaps she refused to comply. He then decided to murder her to keep her quiet, or at best, to do her an injury to show what he was capable of.'

'But why risk it in front of so many people?' asked McPherson. 'Why not just come up to her in a dark alley and do it?'

'There is, I believe, something in the legal profession called "plausible deniability"' said Shaw tentatively. 'I seem to recall the term being used during the enquiry into that unfortunate business at the Larches.'

Ludd grunted. 'That's the Special Branch case up the road the Christmas before last, that the vicar refuses to let us in on,' he said to McPherson, who raised an eyebrow but said nothing.

Shaw politely ignored the interruption and continued. 'What I mean to say is, Havering may have been "hiding in plain sight", as they say. It was a daring act to attempt to injure, perhaps even to deliberately kill Mrs Hexham in front of a large audience, but that is the beauty of it; nobody would believe that such a daring act would be carried out, because it could be plausibly denied and claimed to be an accident.'

'And a young public-school tyke like Havering with more confidence than sense was vain enough to think he *could* persuade us it was an accident,' mused Ludd. 'Yes, I see what you mean, Mr Shaw.'

'Remember also Mr Havering is an actor,' continued Shaw. 'A good one, from what I have seen. A practiced seducer, it seems also. Able to convince others whenever he wishes to get his way.'

'He might have got away with it too, if the business about the London doctor hadn't come out,' said Ludd, shaking his head. 'All right, I've heard enough. McPherson, get on the telephone to Midchester and start the arrangements for a remand hearing with the magistrates. I think we've found our killer.'

A short time later, Shaw stood alone in the village hall, its dusty, locked-up silence in stark contrast to the bustling life and noise of the day before. Ludd and McPherson had left after a final examination of the stage, taking the torn and blood-stained curtain with them as evidence.

Shaw had asked if he might pray near to to the site of Mrs Hexham's demise; Ludd had exhibited his usual faint embarrassment that Shaw had noticed he displayed whenever religious topics were raised, but he had complied with the request.

After a strict admonition from the caretaker to secure the night-latch on the door when he departed, to protect the premises against reporters, he was left alone.

He sat at the prompter's table and prayed briefly, asking for strength for those affected to carry on, and for justice to be done. He then looked up to the stage. He could see on the boards the dried bloodstain marking the place where Mrs Hexham had fallen; in his mind's eye he saw her head turning to stage right, facing the chaise longue on which Madame Dubois had sat.

She had said something after she fell; he had not been sure before but now that he had a chance to view the scene again, it came back to him. He had not heard the words, but in his mind's eye he clearly saw her head turned in the direction of the elegant Belgian woman in her line of sight, and he saw Mrs Hexham's lips move as if she might well have uttered the words 'you traitor'.

Ludd steered his car carefully past a pair of shire horses plodding in front of a brewer's dray on the main road to Midchester, hoping none of their muck had got on the inside of the mudguards.

He could, of course, have driven Havering himself to the station in Midchester, but the thought of transporting criminals in his new car, the same car he was using to squire his wife around in, filled him with distaste, and he had telephoned for another car to be despatched to collect the man from the village police house.

He felt momentarily satisfied with himself, having managed to close a major case in less than 24 hours; then felt a slight emptiness as he remembered the dozen or so other cases, most of them tedious, predictable or downright dull, awaiting his response when he returned to the station. Then there would be the long quiet evening at home, in the too-empty house…

He turned to McPherson, who was gazing at the scenery. 'You thought any more about my offer?' he asked.

McPherson turned away from the window to face the Chief Inspector. 'Aye, sir, I almost forgot to tell you.'

'Well?'

'It's yes. Jean liked the idea.'

'Right then. Move in next week?'

'Ah…there's a wee problem wi' that, sir.'

'Oh yes?'

'The auld dragon of a landlady was waiting for me when I came home late last night. Ticked me off terrible. Said it was no' respectable coming home that late in such a good street.'

Ludd raised an eyebrow. 'Respectable? The bobbies patrol in pairs down that street.'

'Anyways,' continued McPherson, 'I was'nae having that, so I cut her short and told her exactly what I thought o' her and her "respectability".'

'Oh dear,' said Ludd with a chuckle.

'So from tomorrow we're out on the streets.'

'You timed that well,' said Ludd. 'Got much stuff to move?'

'Nah, only a few cases and trunks and things. Most are packed anyway.'

'Move in tomorrow then. I'll bring the car round.'

'Thank you sir. Oh there's just one condition.'

'Oh yes? And what might that be? You're not going to start haggling about the rent, are you?'

'No. It's on the condition that Jean does the housework. She says she would'nae feel right doing nothing about the place.'

'Hmm. I don't think Mrs Ludd would stand for another woman doing all her housework. I mentioned getting a servant and she hit the roof. How about a compromise? Fifty-fifty. Share the work between them.'

'Aye, that sounds all right, sir. I think she'll agree.'

Ludd slowed the car down as they approached the busy crossroads at the outskirts of Midchester; a white-gloved police constable on traffic duty initially held the car up with a hand signal, but then when he saw the occupants, the signal quickly turned to a salute and he stopped the traffic in the opposite direction to allow them to pass through.

'What's sauce for the goose is sauce for the gander though, son,' said Ludd.

'What's that, sir?' said McPherson with a puzzled expression.

'Fifty-fifty for the ladies with the housework, and fifty-fifty for the men with the gardening. How are you at weeding? I can't stand the blasted job.'

'What do we know of Madame Dubois?' asked Shaw of his wife. They were in the little chintzy sitting room of the vicarage drinking coffee, after they had finished lunch and Hettie had been safely dispatched to the kitchen. The couple's little West Highland terrier, Fraser, slept contentedly on the floor at Shaw's feet.

'Not a great deal,' said Mrs Shaw thoughtfully. 'She's not one of us, of course.'

'Us?'

'I mean she's a Catholic. They all are in Belgium, I think.'

'I meant rather her background. Her past.'

'Very little. Dubois is her maiden name, I know that. She's a widow, and was married to an Englishman. Haskins, or Hoskins, was his name, I think. Not exactly top-drawer, but plenty of money, I seem to recall. She has a boy at a boarding school somewhere. Nowhere particularly grand. Chillingborough, I think.'

Shaw sipped his coffee and smiled at his wife's never failing ability to notice the minutest details of social status, somehow without ever taking them too seriously.

'I do seem to recall something about some sort of scandal,' said Mrs Shaw, frowning. 'But then you know how village people can talk, especially when it concerns a foreigner, and a glamorous female one at that.'

'Glamorous?' asked Shaw.

'Oh come along Lucian,' said his wife. 'Even you must have noticed that.'

'I suppose she is rather smart,' murmured Shaw vaguely. 'But...a scandal, you say?'

'It's probably nothing,' said Mrs Shaw. 'You know how these things go, like that parlour game Chinese Whispers or whatever it's called. The story gets changed in the telling. But there was something a few years ago in the newspapers about her, that's all I heard.'

Shaw filled his pipe distractedly and was about to light it.

'Oh not in here, Lucian,' said his wife. 'You know I love the smell when you're smoking it but it does tend to linger in here and go stale.'

'Of course, of course,' said Shaw, putting his pipe away in his pocket. He stood up; Fraser immediately roused himself and shook his little body violently, then looked up in the expectation of a forthcoming walk.

'I think I ought to do some...parish visiting.'

Mrs Shaw looked at him suspiciously.

'You didn't mention that before. Look here, you're not going off on one of your flights of detective fancy, are you?'

'Why do you think that?' asked Shaw.

'All these questions about Madame. You're up to something. Why, when you told me the police have already decided it was Havering?'

'I merely wish to satisfy myself that they have the right person,' said Shaw, 'in order to reassure my parishioners. I shan't be long.'

'You've got Evening Prayer soon,' said his wife in a tone which suggested that was the end of any possibility of detective work.

'Laithwaite can...' began Shaw, but was then cut off.

'Your poor put-upon curate can *not* take Evening Prayer for you today,' replied Mrs Shaw triumphantly. 'His landlady sent word while you are out; he has a cold. So you will have to take the service after all.'

Shaw sat back down, suitably admonished. He decided to put his curiosity about Madame Dubois to one side, at least until tomorrow.

The following afternoon Shaw found himself in front of Madame Dubois' little boutique in the village high street; a small timber-fronted shop with a bay window displaying fur coats and other winter apparel. Before he could enter, a young woman emerged from the door and almost bumped in to him.

'Sorry vicar,' said the young woman gaily. 'I'm in a bit of a rush.'

Shaw looked at the girl, who was dressed in a cheap but fetching cloche hat and woollen winter coat with some sort of fur trimmings. He recognised her as one of the cast members from the play, the one courting PC Arbon, and raised his hat.

'It's, ah, Miss Garrod, I think?'

'That's right,' replied the young woman. 'Saw you at the village hall. Terrible to-do, weren't it?'

'Indeed,' said Shaw. 'But at least the police now have a suspect in custody.'

'Yes, that Ronnie – who would have thought it, eh?'

'Quite. Have you been browsing at Madame's shop?'

'Me?' tittered Miss Garrod. 'Not my sort of style, them old things,' she said. 'No, I chars for Madame. Tidying the shop, and that. Just finished now. Did you want to see her?'

'Yes,' replied Shaw. 'A pastoral visit. I am hoping to

speak to everyone involved in the sad business the other night. It will have upset people greatly.'

'I'll say,' said Miss Garrod. 'Some of the other girls in the group are heart-broken. They thought Ronnie – Mr Havering I mean – was as good as Valentino. But *I* always thought as he was a wrong un. The type what loves you and leaves you, if you know what I mean.'

'One never can tell,' murmured Shaw.

'You're in luck today though,' said Miss Garrod. 'Today's early closing, that's when I cleans the place.'

She looked at her wristwatch. 'Normally Madame shuts up shop by now of a Wednesday and goes to see Mrs Hexham at 'ome. But, well, she can't do that anymore can she?' she asked sadly.

'Madame was friends with Mrs Hexham?' asked Shaw.

'Well, I wouldn't say friends as such,' said Miss Garrod. 'Mrs H wasn't the sort to have 'em – friends that is – if you know what I mean – but they got on all right I think. Must have done. Said Mrs Hexham helped her with how to say her lines in the play, on account of her being a Belgiumer, and not talking English proper. So she can't have been all bad, that Mrs Hexham, can she?

'There is good and bad in all of us,' said Shaw, then frowned in distaste at his own platitude. He found making polite conversation with young women like Miss Garrod something of a trial, and resolved to end the conversation.

He did not need an excuse, as at that moment the doorbell clanged and Madame Dubois appeared at the door.

'Have you forgotten something, Iris?' she asked.

'No Madame, just got chatting to the vicar 'ere,' she replied gaily. 'I'll be off now then. Cheerio Madame. Ta-ta, vicar.'

'Ta...er, good day,' said Shaw, and raised his hat again.

Miss Garrod sashayed off along the pavement, the metal tips of her little high-heels clacking as she went.

'May I help you?' enquired Madame Dubois.

Shaw raised his hat once more. 'Good afternoon,' he said. 'I wonder if I might come in? I shall not be long – I am paying visits to those involved in the recent...unfortunate events, to see if I may be of any assistance.'

Madame Dubois opened the door wider and gestured for him to come in. She closed the door and turned the sign hanging on it to indicate that the shop was closed.

Shaw stood in the centre of the little shop, feeling somewhat uncomfortable in such highly feminine surroundings, claustrophobic with its tightly packed rails of coats and dresses, with hats, gloves and bags exhibited on seemingly every surface.

'I dislike this early closing,' said Madame Dubois. 'It seems a waste of time to me, but, what can one do? It is the custom of the land.'

'At least you were able to use the time constructively,' said Shaw. 'Miss Garrod mentioned you were in the habit of visiting Mrs Hexham on half-days and that she helped you with your lines for the play.'

'My lines?' asked Madame Dubois. 'Ah, yes. She is talkative, that girl. A good worker, though.'

'It was kind of Mrs Hexham to offer to help you in that way,' said Shaw. 'I expect you will miss her.'

'I will not pretend that I liked her,' sniffed Madame Dubois. 'A person can be helpful and unpleasant at the same time. But I would not wish such a death on anyone,' she added. 'The police have arrested Ronald Havering, I see from the newspaper.'

'Yes,' said Shaw simply.

'I think you know the police quite well, yes?' asked Madame Dubois. 'Do they know what was his *motif*?'

'His motive?' replied Shaw. 'They believe that he may have been enraged by a letter that Mrs Hexham sent him, and that he decided either to kill or injure her in revenge.'

'It is as I thought,' said Madame Dubois as she listlessly rearranged a pile of gloves on the glass-fronted counter of the shop. 'He is a very passionate young man, I think. The opposite of Mrs Hexham. Unhelpful, but pleasant. The sort of man that knows how to make a woman feel as if she is the most beautiful one of all in the room. There are not many Englishmen such as that. He has…how you say…*charme*. It is a pity he will surely be hunged.'

Shaw frowned. It never ceased to amaze him how men of Havering's type were able to beguile so many women into admiring them. He chose his next words carefully.

'I believe you also received a letter.'

'I did and I said this to the police also,' said Madame Dubois briskly. 'It was of no consequence to anyone. And please do not ask to see it. Ronnie has been arrested, the killer has been found, and the matter is over.'

'Of course,' replied Shaw. 'I can see you are a strong woman, Madame Dubois,' he continued, 'and have little need of moral support. I should be getting on to others that may require counsel; but please do not hesitate to call at the vicarage should you require help in any way.'

'That is most kind,' said Madame Dubois as she showed Shaw out. 'But as you say, I have no need of the moral supports.'

In his neat little Tudor cottage close to the River Midwell on the outskirts of Lower Addenham, Clarence Weekes poured himself his third stiff whisky of the day.

Carefully groomed and dressed in a well-cut lounge suit with a brightly coloured bow tie, even though he had no company but his own, he paced up and down his little sitting room past the cabinet holding his collection of Tournai porcelain.

He had taken three days off work, as he found the three night run that was normal for the LADS performances to be rather tiring. Of course, there were not going to be any performances now; there had been some vague murmurings about a postponement but nobody really seemed in the mood to discuss it, especially now since their leading man was out of the picture. Weekes was thus at something of a loose end, and had spent his free time fretting and endlessly going over Mrs Hexham's death in his mind.

He sat down in a chintz armchair and picked up the newspaper to read through the article again. It was headed 'Village hall slaying: man charged.'

It was the fourth or fifth time he had read the article; he had lost count. But there it was: 'Ronald Charles Havering, 25, of Kenilworth Lodge, Lower Addenham, Suffolk, has been charged with the murder of…'

He could hardly believe it, and read through the article once more. He took a sip of whisky; there had been no further questioning from the police and they had accepted on face value, it seemed, his lie about not having received a letter from Mrs Hexham.

It really seemed, he thought to himself with a growing sense of relief, that he was no longer of any interest to the police.

His relief was short-lived; he heard the rattle of the

door-knocker and jumped slightly; nerves, he realised; was it the police? He held his breath.

He looked carefully out of the little leaded bay window, expecting to see the two detectives that had been at the village hall the other night; then he exhaled noisily. It was only the vicar.

Weekes felt quite glad of the visit; the isolated cottage was lonely at the best of times; he suddenly longed for the company of his work companions, whom he normally found somewhat tedious.

He showed Shaw into the little sitting room.

'A beautiful collection of porcelain,' said Shaw, looking at the glass cabinet by the door. 'Sevres?'

'Tournai, from Belgium,' said Weekes. 'I find Sevres a little too garish.'

'Quite so,' said Shaw. 'I have no real knowledge of fine china. Mrs Shaw does not trust me with anything other than the most solid and plain Staffordshire ware.'

'On that subject, may I offer you something, vicar?' asked Weekes. 'A cup of tea, or something stronger perhaps? I'm afraid I've already started on whisky. Settles the nerves, you see.'

'Ah, a little early for me,' said Shaw, 'and I shan't put you to the trouble of making tea as I do not wish to take up too much of your time. I felt however I ought to visit those involved in the recent terrible event at the village hall, particularly one such as yourself who makes such a splendid contribution to our church choir.'

'Involved?' asked Weekes quickly. Perhaps too quickly, he thought, and took a deep breath to calm himself.

'Yes, those who were the principal witnesses,' said Shaw as he sat down on the little William Morris print sofa.

'I told the police I didn't see anything,' said Weekes emphatically. 'It was dark behind that curtain.'

'Of course, of course,' said Shaw. 'But you will of course have to appear at the inquest, and eventual trial, and I wanted to assure you of my moral support in that regard.'

'Trial?' said Weekes, as he paced up and down the room. 'But I tell you, I didn't see anything. They've got Havering for it, what do they need me for?'

'It may perhaps not come to that, you are right,' said Shaw. 'Madame Dubois and myself, my wife and Mr Hexham were the only others in close enough proximity to be of interest to the police, and we may be sufficient witnesses for a court case. It is too early to tell.'

'There must have been fifty people in that hall, they all must have seen that Havering did it,' said Weekes.

'Chief Inspector Ludd believes the audience were too far away to have seen anything of use in a court of law. The pianist was facing the wrong way, and so did not see anything either.'

'But they don't need me in court, do they?' said Weekes quickly. 'Digging things up, cross-examining...' he realised he was jabbering, and stopped talking.

'My dear chap, you have gone quite pale,' said Shaw. 'Please do sit down. Have another glass of whisky, do not hold back on my account.'

'Thanks, I will,' said Weekes, then wondered why he was thanking someone for offering him his own refreshments. He poured a stiff whisky and splashed rather too much soda from the syphon; he fussily wiped the drops from his shirt-front with his handkerchief.

'That will do you good,' said Shaw. 'Now, I shall not trouble you any further.' Weekes saw with relief that Shaw was getting up to go.

Before he closed the door on him, Shaw turned and said 'I shall be praying for you, Mr Weekes.'

Weekes felt a pang of guilt and fear. Did the vicar know

something? He was looking at him intently; Weekes recalled the man had seemed awfully pally with that detective fellow the other night.

'Don't worry about me, vicar,' said Weekes quickly. 'It's the real sinners like Havering who need your prayers more than me.'

'"All have sinned and come short of the glory of God", Mr Weekes,' quoted Shaw with a smile. 'I shall be praying for you *both*.'

Weekes was about to shut the door, but found he could not help himself from speaking.

'Look here, vicar…'

Shaw paused on the threshold of the cottage's ancient front door.

'Yes?'

'Do you think that if somebody did something…very wrong, but somehow got away with it, that would be, well, very wrong also?'

'Indeed it would.'

'Ah…'

'Mr Weekes, is there something you wish to tell me about?'

Weekes shook his head violently.

'No, not at all,' he said, slurring his words slightly. 'But I mean, that is to say, we ought to come clean about things, oughtn't we? People in general, I mean.'

'Every church service begins with just such an admonition, Mr Weekes, as I am sure you know.'

'Yes…yes of course,' murmured Weekes. '"Followed too much the devices and desires of our own hearts", and all that.' He suddenly felt cautious; the whisky had made him far too talkative.

'Well that's put my mind at rest,' he said to Shaw, managing a weak smile.

Shaw looked at Weekes quizzically. 'Do call at the vicarage if you should wish to talk further,' he said. 'At any time.'

'No need, no need,' said Weekes hurriedly. 'Thanks all the same vicar. Goodnight.'

'Goodnight.'

Weekes almost slammed the door and gulped down the remainder of the whisky in his glass.

Chapter Eight

Later that afternoon Shaw sat in his study, puffing on his pipe and vainly attempting to compose his sermon for the following Sunday. He knew he ought to mention the death of Mrs Hexham, but he disliked using the pulpit to disseminate local news, lest he gain a reputation for transmitting gossip; he decided instead to concentrate on the theme of mortality and the shortness of life.

He looked once again at the appointed gospel for inspiration, leafing through the heavy leather-bound bible at his desk, its pages mellowed with age and infused with the scent of pipe tobacco, the product of countless bowls he had smoked while reading it, offered up like incense.

The gospel for next Sunday was that of St Matthew, chapter 27, but he found his eye leading him on from the appointed verse to a later section. Verse 51:

> And behold, the veil of the temple was rent in twain from top to bottom, and the earth did quake, and the rocks rent...

He rubbed his eyes; several thoughts and theories were jostling in his mind at once and he longed for clarity. Suddenly a thought occurred to him, and he stood up and walked into the hall. Fraser followed him, his tail wagging as he expected a walk, but his little face showed disappointment when Shaw bundled him back into the study. He checked for something in the pocket of his overcoat, which was hanging on the hall-stand, and then picked up the telephone and asked for a Midchester number. After a few moments, he was connected.

'Is that the *Evening News*?' he enquired. 'May I speak to Mr Fred Gutteridge?'

In the bowels of Midchester police station, Ludd and McPherson sat at a scarred wooden table in a gloomy basement room, its brick walls painted dark green to a height of four feet, and off-white thereafter upwards to the low ceiling; set high in the wall was a barred window which looked out onto the street above; the only view observable was the lower legs of the occasional passer-by.

This had occasioned interest in some prisoners, hoping for a glimpse of something more than a woman's well-turned ankle as she walked past, but the sensible Victorian architect who designed the building had placed a brick awning over the exterior of the window, ensuring that no passer-by could ever walk close enough for the necessary voyeuristic angle of vision within the cell.

Ronald Havering, who sat opposite the two detectives, exhibited no interest in the window nor anything else in the room. He smoked listlessly, staring into middle distance; next to him an efficient-looking man in morning dress, with slim aristocratic features and a neatly trimmed moustache, shuffled papers on top of a briefcase, which was one of the finest articles on offer from Messrs Swaine and Adeney of St James.

The man, who was none other than Sir John Ellison,

King's Counsel, consulted an ancient and battered gold pocket-watch which he withdrew solemnly from his dove-grey waistcoat.

'If there are no further questions, I should like to go,' he drawled. 'I have a train leaving shortly.'

Ludd noticed with annoyance that the man's phrasing suggested the train was his own personal conveyance. He had met Sir John's sort before and the one thing that one did not do with the likes of him, was to show any sort of annoyance. That made them think they'd got the better of you, and, thought Ludd, I am not having *that*.

Havering's solicitor had been bad enough, but then this stuck-up individual, a noted barrister, had appeared and started questioning all sorts of things to do to with Ludd's handling of the case. The man knew Havering's father – McPherson had heard him mentioned when he searched Havering's room – and was trying to get the police to drop the murder charge.

'We accept the charge of abetment with regards to the…illegal medical procedure,' said Sir John with distaste, 'but let me assure you it is highly unlikely Mr Havering will be prosecuted in this matter. The girl, on the other hand…'

'The girl has'nae got a fancy lawyer looking after her,' snapped McPherson. 'She's on remand in the women's gaol probably wondering why the hell she bothered telling anyone about all this.'

'As I was saying,' continued Sir John calmly, ignoring McPherson completely, 'we do accept that charge. The charge of murder of Mrs, ah, Hexham, however, is preposterous. I shall be speaking to the Chief Constable personally about this.'

'I expect you know him?' asked Ludd, doing his best to to reveal no emotion. 'Same club? Or do you ride to hounds together?'

'We are acquainted,' said Sir John simply. 'Quite frankly I am amazed that the police expect to prosecute such a flimsy case. If Scotland Yard were involved....'

'Well Scotland Yard is *not* involved,' said Ludd, 'and nor will they be, unless my governor gets told by *his* governor – that's your pal the Chief Constable – that they *are* involved. Until then you've got me to deal with, and we're going ahead with the charge of murder.'

Ludd folded his arms and looked the barrister straight in the eye. There was a moment of silence.

'Very well...' began Sir John.

'It's ludicrous!' exclaimed Havering, and smacked his hand down on the table; the burning tip of the cigarette he was holding detached itself and flew on to Sir John's papers; the barrister fussily flicked the embers away and turned to his client.

'I have already advised you to...'

'To keep bloody quiet,' interrupted McPherson angrily. 'Aye, we know, and you can keep still as well. Any more banging like that and you'll have the cuffs back on and nae cigarettes either.'

'I'm sorry,' breathed Havering, although everything in his manner suggested he was not at all sorry. 'But the whole thing is preposterous. Why pick on me? The others all got letters, they all hated Mrs Hexham...'

'Aye but they didnae stab her in full view of witnesses,' said McPherson with a sigh.

'Wait a minute, who are "the others" and how do you know they all got letters?' asked Ludd.

'Look,' said Havering emphatically. 'They must have done. I got a letter. The Cranstons got one, and so did Madame Dubois.'

'How did you know that?' asked McPherson.

'I'm not deaf,' said Havering. 'I could hear your Chief Inspector talking while you babysat me at the side of the stage.'

'Weekes didn't get a letter,' said Ludd.

'Think not?' said Havering with a smile. 'I'm pretty sure he did. I saw him in the dressing room looking at a letter that was pretty similar to the one I got. Greenish paper, dense handwriting. His face looked a picture. How do you know it wasn't him substituted that dagger and got me to stab old Mrs Hexham without realising it?'

'Mr Havering, you ought to have mentioned this before,' said Sir John. 'It could have a bearing on the case.'

'Nobody bothered to ask me,' replied the young man. 'These two are already convinced I did it.'

'Now look here,' said Ludd. 'I've made a note of what you...claim...about Weekes getting a letter. But that doesn't mean much. We've tested those two daggers and anyone holding the real one for more than few seconds would know it was real by the feel of it. So don't start trying to pin blame on others with talk of letters and substituting things.'

There was a moment of silence; Havering sat back in his chair, folded his arms and stared into middle distance. A tram rumbled and clanged on the street above, and Sir John stood up.

'I shall return for the remand hearing tomorrow,' he said to Havering. 'I will also be consulting with the detectives at Scotland Yard dealing with the other charge.'

'Give them my love, won't you?' said Ludd.

'Good day, gentlemen,' said Sir John blandly.

After the lawyer had left and Havering had been returned to his cell, Ludd tapped his indelible pencil slowly on the scarred surface of the table.

McPherson broke the silence. 'Do you think he's telling

the truth about seeing Weekes with a letter?'

'Don't see why he'd lie about it, as it doesn't do *him* much good,' said Ludd. 'I don't see that it matters much anyway. Havering's still the only one to have actually stabbed the deceased.'

'Aye,' said McPherson. 'Bit shifty of this Weekes to lie about no' getting a letter.'

'We don't know he even did get a letter from Mrs Hexham,' said Ludd. 'It could have been his milk bill he was looking at. Havering's probably just trying to cast aspersions, lay a false trail for us or just waste our blasted time on wild goose chases. That said, I think I'd like you to speak to our Mr Weekes again and warn him about withholding evidence.'

'Right sir. I'll go tomorrow.'

'Tomorrow? Why not today?'

'You gave me the afternoon off. To move our things from the flat. You said you'd pick us up in your car.'

'So I did. I was forgetting you're moving in with us today. Mrs Ludd's been talking about nothing else, she's been cleaning nooks and crannies in that house I never knew existed. Go tomorrow then.'

'Thank you sir,' said McPherson, then paused. 'That barrister said the case was weak. And he's a King's Counsel. Do you no' think…'

Ludd raised his hand.

'I don't care,' he said, 'if Sir John High and Mighty is a King's Counsel or a County Council, he's not coming in here telling me how to do my job. So while you're in Lower Addenham, speak to as many of the witnesses and the people who were backstage and so on as you can. Speak to Reverend Shaw again, see if he knows any gossip. Get anything you can on bad feeling between Havering and Mrs Hexham. We need to make sure we can prove he had it in for her.'

'Right sir.'

Ludd coughed to hide his embarrassment. 'Oh, and by the way, ah...when we're off duty, around the house and so on...there's no need to call me sir. George will do. And I'll call you James, if I may. I'll wait for Mrs Ludd to invite you to use her Christian name though, if you don't mind.'

'Thank you s...I mean, thank you George,' said McPherson.

'We're still on duty, lad.'

'Sorry, sir.'

Ludd grinned. 'Come on, get your hat and coat, I'll bring the pantechnicon round.'

Shaw walked into the taproom of the George, the larger of Lower Addenham's two public houses, which also doubled as a small hotel. It was named in honour of the first King George, having been built shortly after his accession in 1714, but had been extensively renovated in the 1920s and now resembled a pastiche Elizabethan inn.

At this time of day, outside official licensing hours, the bar room was deserted, being open only to hotel guests who were permitted to purchase alcohol at any time.

Shaw soon saw the man he was looking for, and sat down opposite him at a corner table.

'Good afternoon, Mr Gutteridge,' he said.

The *Midchester Evening News* reporter nodded, but did not get up.

'How do, vicar,' he said. 'Care for a glass of beer? They do a good drop of mild here.'

He gestured to a pint glass on the table, and Shaw

noticed there was also a small glass of whisky next to it, with another empty whisky glass beside that one.

'They're not open yet,' said Shaw. 'How did you manage that? You're not a guest, are you?'

Gutteridge tapped the side of his somewhat red nose. 'Don't need to be. *Bona fide* traveller, aren't I? Told 'em I got a right to service.'

'But you've come from Midchester, that's only four miles away,' replied Shaw.

'They don't know that, do they?' said the journalist. 'What'll it be?'

'Nothing, thank you,' said Shaw. He disliked such petty infringements of the law, mainly because he did not want the village pub's licence to be put at risk simply to satisfy the thirst of a non-resident.

'What have you got for me, then?' asked Gutteridge eagerly. 'You didn't say much on the telephone.'

'Local telephone exchanges have ears,' said Shaw, tapping his nose also. 'And forgive me for not inviting you to the vicarage, but if any others of your profession were watching they might think something was "going on".'

'What exactly *is* going on, vicar?' said Gutteridge, downing his second whisky of the day.

'I wish to offer you what I believe is known in the newspaper world as an "exclusive",' said Shaw. 'A statement about what I saw on the night of Mrs Hexham's death.'

'Cor, a scoop,' said Gutteridge, leaning forward and grabbing his notebook and pencil from his raincoat pocket. 'I'm all ears, vicar.'

'One moment,' said Shaw. 'This is not an act of charity. I do expect something in return.'

Gutteridge groaned. 'Look here, vicar, I thought better of a man of the cloth. I'll see what I can do but it won't be much. Two pound ten, a fiver at the most. Depends on what sort of juicy details you can...'

Shaw interrupted the reporter by raising his hand. 'I do not want money in exchange. What I would like is some information from your newspaper cuttings library.'

The dusk was gathering as Shaw left the George; Gutteridge's little car whizzed away up the road to Midchester, the horn tootling as it passed by. The sky over the distant fields was tinged with a yellowish orange; a few starlings chirrupped in the trees and Shaw could smell a mixture of coal and wood smoke as the kitchen ranges of the village began to be lighted for supper.

Shaw let himself in to the vicarage, and once he had ascertained from Hettie that his wife was still out visiting a sick parishioner, he took his briefcase from the hall stand and climbed the stairs to the first floor. He opened the large, dark-wood linen cupboard on the landing.

A smell of furniture polish and dried lavender greeted him; he felt uneasy intruding into this feminine domain. Carefully he examined the piles of neatly folded sheets and pillowcases until he found what he was looking for; an old, heavily darned bedsheet. He extracted it carefully from the pile and placed it in his briefcase, then set off down the hill to the village hall.

After a few moments of tedious wrangling with the caretaker, he was able to borrow the latch-key and let himself in to the hall. He first checked the notice board with its type-written notice of days and times of events being held in the hall; the Mother's Union, the Knitting Circle, the Chess Club and so on. He satisfied himself that no meetings were due in the next half-hour or so, and crossed the hall to the stage.

It had now been cleaned, he noticed, and no trace of Mrs Hexham's blood remained on the boards; only a slightly lighter patch where the wood had been scrubbed was visible. He looked up, and saw with relief that the wire which had held the curtain through which Mrs Hexham had been stabbed was still in place.

He unfolded the bedsheet he had brought with him and, with some difficulty, managed to hang it over the wire, as if he were hanging washing on the line. It looked, as well as he could remember, much the same as the sheet which had been in place on the night of the play.

He then went to the row of round bakelite switches on the wall near the front door of the hall and flicked them on and off until he had reached an approximation of the light level in the hall on the night of the killing. An idea struck him, and he took the little table lamp from the desk in front of the stage, which he had used to illuminate his prompter's script, and directed it to the stage as a kind of spotlight. As far as he could recall, the scene now looked very similar to how it had appeared on the night of the fateful performance.

He climbed on to the stage and shuffled behind the improvised curtain, and stood between it and the wooden flats which had been painted to appear like stonework. He looked around the claustrophobic space and frowned, his brow furrowed with marks of deep concern.

'Glass of beer before supper, James?' said Ludd to McPherson, who stood awkwardly in the Chief Inspector's sitting room. 'The way your wife and mine are nattering away in the kitchen I can see it'll be a while before anything's ready.'

'Aye, thank you s...er, George,' said McPherson. 'Thirsty work, this moving.'

'All done now though, eh?' said Ludd, as he took a bottle of brown ale from a little cupboard in the corner of the room and poured out a glassful.

'That's called a "cocktail cabinet", would you believe it,' said Ludd, as he handed the foaming glass to the sergeant. 'Mrs Ludd...Mildred, that is, bought it from Corder's. I'd no idea what a cocktail was, if truth be told. Thought it might be part of a chicken's anatomy, but it's some sort of American drink apparently.'

'I prefer beer myself,' said McPherson.

'Same here. Well, here's how.'

'Cheers.'

'Here,' said Ludd, 'if you like a good drop of beer, they do a decent pint at the Haywain up the road. We could go after supper.'

'Thanks all the same, but I'm a wee bit tired,' said McPherson.

'Well, there's boxing on the wireless later,' said Ludd. 'We could have a listen to that, and stay in.'

'If it's all the same to you I'll have an early night,' said McPherson. 'Got a lot of questioning to do tomorrow.'

'Of course,' said Ludd. He suspected he was overwhelming the man. The domestic arrangement, although mutually beneficial, was going to take a little bit of getting used to, he decided, so he ought to go easy on the lad.

The rather awkward silence was broken by the sound of the telephone bell from the hallway.

'Now who can that be?' asked Ludd. 'It'll have to be the

horticultural society chap this time. It's all right mother, I'll get it,' he called to his wife, who had begun to emerge from the kitchen.

Ludd picked up the instrument and announced his telephone exchange and number.

'Yes, this is he,' he replied to the caller with a sigh. He knew that since this young female telephonist had addressed him as Chief Inspector, that the call was going to be of an official nature.

'Police mortuary?' he said. 'What do they want at this time of night? The doctor? Ah yes, it's quite all right, I did say he could call me at home when he'd finished the post-mortem. Can you put him through? Right you are.'

Ludd greeted the police doctor cautiously and listened to him for a few moments; his face darkening with concern.

'You're absolutely sure about that?' he enquired emphatically. 'No possibility of a mistake? Right. I see, thank you doctor. Yes, yes, she's well thank you. Yes I'll pass on your regards. Goodnight.'

Ludd grabbed his hat and coat from the hall stand and took McPherson's as well. He entered the sitting room and tossed the items of clothing at the sergeant.

'Here, catch these as well,' he said, throwing a set of keys. 'Know how to drive, don't you?'

'Aye, but what's going…' started McPherson.

'Bring my car out of the garage and onto the road. Keep the engine running. I've some telephone calls to make in the meantime. Something's come up.'

'But what…'

'I'll tell you later. Just bring the Austin round. Watch the gates, it's a tight squeeze and if you mark that car I'll mark you!'

Shaw left the village hall and returned the key to the caretaker, dropping it through his letterbox rather than have to reassure the rather surly man in person that he had indeed switched off the electric lights and locked the door properly.

It was dark now, and a few lights had come on in the cottages nearby; bright in some places where electricity was laid on, and a softer, dimmer glow in those rooms where only oil lamps were in use. A frost had already begun to form, and the grass verge in front of the village hall on which Shaw now stood appeared grey in the waxing moonlight.

He gazed into the distance beyond the village. The stars were now clearly visible over the whole sky; beneath them, as far as he could see, were the barren dunes of the winter fields, laid out like a giant patchwork quilt towards the shingled desolation of the North Sea coast, far out of view. Was this, thought Shaw, what the surface of the moon felt like? A cold, dark, sterile emptiness, stretching onward until it merged into the infinite darkness of space?

From the corner of his eye he saw a figure; a man walking slowly up the high street with what looked like a shotgun bag on his shoulder. Shaw strained his eyes but could not make out his features; it seemed the man turned to look at him, but did not acknowledge him, and continued walking. Shaw shrugged; he was not sure if it was a friend, and it was too far to call simply 'good evening' to someone who might be a stranger.

He took a sharp intake of breath and exhaled with a

plume of vapour. Too much pondering, he decided. He considered the matter in hand and wondered what to do. Ought he to telephone Ludd? The Chief Inspector had, after all, given him his home number, but it was after business hours and he did not like to bother him.

Ludd had already dismissed Shaw's concerns about the meaning of Mrs Hexham's last words. Ought he to speak to PC Arbon perhaps, at the village police house? No, a bad idea. The man was new to the job, and, even if he agreed to help, he might perhaps ruin a delicate situation.

Seeing the dim light of the telephone kiosk at the bottom of the high street, he decided that he would after all try to speak to Ludd. Fumbling for pennies in his trouser pocket, at the same time he fished out the little business card with the man's telephone number on it, and asked the operator to put him through.

Yes, said a loud but uncertain female voice, this was the home of Chief Inspector George Ludd, but no, he was not at home. This was his wife, Mrs George Ludd. To whom was she speaking? Reverend Shaw? Ah, his name had been mentioned favourably in the Ludd residence on several occasions. No, she did not know when he would return; he had been called away on urgent business the location of which he had not divulged, and she did not know when he would return. She hoped that before long she would have the pleasure of making his acquai…the line went dead as the last of Shaw's pennies was swallowed by the telephone.

Shaw replaced the telephone receiver. He took a deep breath and left the kiosk, and began walking briskly towards the home of Clarence Weekes.

'I ought to get a bell installed on this thing,' said Ludd as he overtook a steam-lorry chugging along the near-empty expanse of the new Midchester bypass. 'Too many slowcoaches in the way.'

'It's no' a police car G...I mean, sir,' said McPherson. 'You've no right of way.'

'I know, I know,' said Ludd, as he squinted through the windscreen. 'Now where's the bally turning? Ah, there it is.'

At a black and white striped signpost marked 'Great Netley 2, Lower Addenham 4, Addenham Magna 5½', Ludd executed a sharp turn. The tyres of the Austin screeched slightly on the tarmac, and then made a whooshing sound as they connected with the loose gravel of the minor road. He struggled with the steering wheel for a moment and then slowed down.

'Going to tell me what this is all about?' enquired McPherson. 'That beer'll be flat if we don't get back soon.'

'Never mind, I'll get you another,' said Ludd. 'That was the police doctor on the telephone. He finally got round to doing the post-mortem on Mrs Hexham.'

'That took him long enough.'

'Been a spate of suicides in Midchester,' said Ludd, 'said our Mrs Hexham had to wait in a queue as it wasn't officially a murder investigation. I should have chivvied him along but well, anyway, too late now.'

'What was so important that we've got to drive out to Addenham in a big rush?' asked McPherson.

'The doctor found out...damned fool!'

Ludd braked hard as a farm labourer on a bicycle pulled out of a side lane and then pedalled slowly across the road towards another turn-off.

Ludd pressed the klaxon, but the labourer continued his

slow pace, pausing only to make an insolent gesture with the fingers of his right hand.

'Oh, very nice,' said Ludd.

McPherson started to open the passenger door but Ludd clapped his hand on the sergeant's arm.

'Leave the gormless idiot, we haven't time,' said Ludd, accelerating sharply once the road was clear.

'Anyway, as I was saying,' said Ludd, 'the doctor told me that after a careful examination, that Mrs Hexham did indeed die from being stabbed.'

'We know that,' said McPherson dismissively.

'Yes, but here's the strange part. She had *two* stab wounds.'

'What the...but we didn't see any other...'

'No, we didn't, because they were in exactly the same place on the abdomen. Doctor said it was only noticeable after careful examination. But she *was* stabbed twice; and not only that, the doctor said it looked like there had been one shallow flesh wound, probably not fatal, and then a second, deeper one into the heart, which was what killed her. We can't be sure but I'm guessing that when Havering stabbed her it wasn't intended to kill her, but the *second* stab was.'

'But Havering only stabbed her the once. Everybody saw that. He couldn't have stabbed her twice.'

'Exactly. Which means the only other person who could have done it was behind that curtain.'

'Who was that? Mr Hexham wasn't it? You're no' saying he killed his own wife?'

'I'm not saying anything. But there was another chap there as well, remember? Clarence Weekes.'

'Of course,' said McPherson, clicking his fingers. 'And he's the one who was shifty, and said he did'nae get a blackmail letter even though Havering said he did.'

'That's the one. I think we need to pay him a little visit, don't you?'

'What about Mr Hexham though? Could he be involved?'

'Possibly, but it seems unlikely. Just in case, I want us to go and have a word with him after we've seen Weekes. While you got the car out, I telephoned to the village police house to get Arbon and that special of his to keep an eye on each of them until we get there.'

Shaw walked purposefully towards Weekes' cottage, resolving to speak to the man to clear the nagging doubts in his mind about something he had said.

The cottage was set back from a small lane off the high street, in a densely wooded spot where the trees, despite being leafless, interwove their branches to form a canopy that blocked much of the moonlight. Shaw saw a chink of light behind the curtains, and breathed a sigh of relief; hopefully the man was still at home.

He opened the little wooden gate and stepped into the garden; gardening, it seemed, was not one of Weekes' interests, as the ground was tussocky and overgrown, with the dead remainders of last year's plants overhanging the path.

He heard a rustling sound behind the ragged hedge on his right, which ran alongside the garden path and marked the boundary of Weekes' property. He stopped and listened, wondering if it might just be the wind, but the night was still and clear. There was another sound, this time of what might be heavy boots on gravel.

Shaw felt his heart begin to pound and he wondered if it

would be best to simply walk on and knock on the cottage door; after all he was doing nothing wrong. But the idea of walking along the path whilst who knew what was behind him did not appeal, and he resolved to find out.

Striking a match, he feigned the lighting of his pipe and took advantage of the brief moment of illumination to look around. He glimpsed a shape through the thin hedge which might have been a man, with an enormous head, standing still; something on his neck or shoulders glinted in the moonlight and then disappeared.

Shaw walked on, and then suddenly turned back and forced his way through the hedge a few feet from the figure.

'Who are you?' he called.

The figure loomed before him.

'I might well ask you the same question,' came a voice from the figure. 'What's your business?'

Shaw suddenly laughed with relief as he realised who it was. The enormous head was a policeman's helmet, and the objects that glinted in the moonlight were his collar numbers.

'Constable Arbon. It is Reverend Shaw.'

'Oh, I'm sorry, vicar,' said Arbon in a low voice. 'Didn't recognise you. Why did you jump through the hedge like that?'

'I…er…saw a figure and was concerned he might be someone up to no good,' said Shaw.

'Hmm,' said Arbon, 'Fair enough. But what brings you down here, may I ask?'

'Parish visiting,' said Shaw. 'I came to see Mr Weekes.'

There was an awkward moment of silence and then the sound of boots on gravel. Both men swung round to see two others approaching, dressed in raincoats and trilby hats.

'What the devil are you doing here, Mr Shaw?' hissed a voice from up the path. It was Chief Inspector Ludd and Sergeant McPherson.

Arbon was now standing to attention and saluting with one hand, while simultaneously trying to extract his bicycle from behind the hedge with the other.

'Oh stand easy, man,' said Ludd with some irritation. 'I sent Arbon here to keep an eye on this cottage as new evidence has come to light, Mr Shaw. Why are *you* down here?'

'For much the same reason,' said Shaw.

'Oh yes, and what have you found out?' asked Ludd.

'Weekes claimed that it was too dark to see anything behind the curtain,' said Shaw. 'But after some…experimentation…in the village hall, I realised this could not have been the case. I decided to come here to ask him about it.'

'Why on earth didn't you telephone me first?' hissed Ludd. 'That's why I gave you my number, to stop you going off and getting yourself into difficulties, which you seem to do rather often.'

'I did try to telephone you, but you were out,' insisted Shaw. 'I wanted to avoid the possibility of Mr Weekes escaping.'

'I'd already thought of that, which is why I posted PC Arbon here to keep an eye on him,' sighed Ludd. 'Anything to report, constable?'

'Nothing sir, well not since I got here a few minutes ago anyway. I think he's in, 'cos his light's on.'

'Right you are,' said Ludd. 'And did you get that Special, what's his name, Tanner, to keep watch on Hexham's house?'

'Yes sir, but he was helping with the lambing up at Top Farm. I managed to get through to them on the telephone but he said he might be a bit late down there.'

'Oh for God's sake...' breathed McPherson.

'Lambs is coming thick and fast now sir,' protested Arbon, 'and Reg – Special Constable Tanner, I mean, he ain't on dooty tonight, so I had a hard job persua...'

'All right, all right, never mind,' said Ludd. 'It's Weekes we need to talk to most of all anyway.'

'May I ask...' began Shaw.

'No you may not Mr Shaw,' said Ludd. 'There isn't time for your speculation. I've a mind to order you home but I'd like to hear more about this "experiment" you carried out in the village hall, so for the moment you can tag along with us.'

The four men walked quietly along the path, with Ludd leading the way. The Chief Inspector indicated for Arbon to go around to the back door, and then rapped sharply on the ancient metal door knocker.

'Mr Weekes,' called Ludd loudly. 'Open up please. It's the police.'

There was no reply, but the door was ajar and swung open under the force of the knock. Shaw began to feel uneasy; Weekes did not seem to be the sort of man who would leave his door unlocked and his lights on if he were not at home.

The three men walked into the little hallway; Ludd called again and again, no reply came.

'McPherson, look in that room there,' said Ludd, pointing to the sitting room. 'Mr Shaw, you come upstairs with me please.'

McPherson disappeared off to the right and Ludd began to climb the little steep flight of stairs to the first floor. Suddenly there was a shout from McPherson.

'Sir, in here, quickly!'

After a brief tussle as Shaw and Ludd tried to turn

round together on the narrow staircase, they entered the sitting room to be confronted by a ghastly sight; the ancient, solid timber beams which criss-crossed the ceiling of the room had been put to a terrible purpose.

Clarence Weekes had hanged himself.

Chapter Nine

'Cheer-oh then.'

'Ta-ta, see you tomorrow.'

'Cheer up, it's Saturday half-day soon!'

These and other expressions typically heard at the close of business in a large workplace echoed around the walls of the *Midchester Evening News* office. Then the last typewriters were covered over and the last hats and coats removed from hooks as their wearers disappeared to tram stops or bicycle sheds to make their weary way home.

Fred Gutteridge, however, was not going home just yet. He was still hard at work in the newspaper archive in the basement, fervently thumbing through index cards, and rifling through stacks of yellowing newspapers.

'Not like you to be in here so late Reg,' said one of the administrators, an elderly man with a green eyeshade and sleeve-garters, who had been directing the reporter to the relevant parts of the library in which to do his research.

'You're usually in the Duke of Norfolk by now, aren't you?' continued the administrator, examining his pocket watch. 'It's gone opening time.'

'Can't,' said Gutteridge, absent-mindedly poking a cigarette into his mouth while he ran a pencil down the column of a faded newspaper, and then made a mark on a notepad next to it.

'Here, no smoking in here,' said the clerk, removing the

unlit cigarette from Gutteridge's mouth for him. 'This place'll go up like a haystack if it catches fire.'

'Sorry Bert,' said Gutteridge. 'This job's taking ages and I'm gasping for a fag.'

'What you looking for?' asked Bert. 'I would help you only we've got a rush job on for that feature on David Lloyd George. Lord knows he's got enough skeletons in cupboards for us to look for.'

'Got a list of some names,' replied Gutteridge, who had little interest at this time in the peccadilloes of former Prime Ministers. 'Trying to find out anything and everything on 'em.'

'I don't envy you,' chuckled Bert. 'As you well know, you can find out almost anything here, but it takes time. Any topics, or names mentioned in every article in every paper of the last few years is noted down and put in those card files, but then you've got to cross-reference it with the actual papers themselves. All the nationals and all the East Anglian papers too. One day I hope they'll invent a quicker way of finding out that sort of information. A machine of some kind, p'raps.'

'Come off it Bert, the union would never allow that,' said Gutteridge with a grim chuckle. 'You'd be out of a job.'

'I'll be long gone by then and the union will probably be gone and all, the way they carry on,' said Bert. 'No, it'll be a machine all right, like one of these adding machines, only it'll work with words instead of numbers, see. Ah, but I'll be in my grave many a year before anything like that happens. Probably take another war, that always seems to speed the inventors up. Anyway, I hope it's worth it. You've been here hours.'

'It's worth it all right. Could be a big scoop.'

'What about?'

'Can't say just yet. Nearly got what I need now and...'

Gutteridge paused and gazed down at an old copy of a Sunday newspaper.

'Bingo!' said Gutteridge. 'That's something on all three names found. Now the vicar has got to give me something good in exchange for this.'

'Vicar?' asked Bert. 'You seen the light, or something?'

Gutteridge, however, was busy tearing a strip off the newspaper and did not answer.

'Here you can't do that, that's company property,' protested Bert.

Gutteridge ignored him, shoved the paper into his raincoat pocket and with a cheery wave disappeared up the stairs in eager expectation of his post-work pint.

Ludd solemnly removed his hat and shook his head slowly as he looked up at Weekes' body dangling from the ceiling of the sitting room.

'Now why on earth did he have to go and do a thing like that,' he said sadly. 'What a way to go.'

Shaw looked at the horror that was Weekes' face, which was red and swollen, almost purple; the man's eyes bulged and looked glassily upwards.

Then his eyes flickered.

'Wait,' said Shaw. 'I think he still may be alive.'

'He's right sir,' said McPherson. 'I just saw his foot twitch.'

'Well don't just stand there, cut him down,' shouted Ludd. 'Arbon, get in here,' he yelled through the French doors. 'Here, Mr Shaw, you help me hold him up. Take the strain off. McPherson, find a knife in the kitchen.'

Shaw and Ludd, now assisted by PC Arbon who had rushed in from the garden, took hold of Weekes' legs and supported him while they listened to McPherson rummaging and crashing cutlery about in the kitchen. Soon he returned, and, placing two upright chairs precariously one on top of the other, was able to reach high enough to cut through the rope around Weekes' neck.

They heaved and strained and eventually managed to get him onto the sofa where he showed dim signs of life, gasping and breathing heavily.

'Brandy!' said Ludd. 'He needs brandy.'

'Certainly not,' insisted Shaw. 'We must not give him anything. We must send for the doctor straight away.'

'You're not a medical man Mr Shaw,' said Ludd. 'I say he needs a good tot to bring him round.'

'I was a medical orderly as part of my chaplaincy work,' said Shaw. 'Brandy may be suitable for a conscious person able to swallow, but for someone in this condition it could be fatal.'

'All right then,' said Ludd. 'McPherson, get on the telephone to the station, tell them to send a doctor.'

'It'll be quicker to fetch the village doctor,' said Arbon. 'Dr Holt. His number's 371.'

'Very well,' said Ludd.

McPherson crossed into the hallway, picked up the telephone and asked the operator for the number; soon afterwards they could hear him speaking in a low but urgent voice to the doctor.

'Oughtn't we to give him artificial resuscitation, or something?' asked Ludd doubtfully, looking down at Weekes on the sofa.

'He is breathing on his own,' said Shaw, examining Weekes' face. A low, gasping, wheezing sound came from the man's mouth but otherwise he showed no signs of life.

'There is little we can do now until the doctor arrives.'

'Looks like he stepped up on one of those chairs, tied the rope up and then kicked it away, poor devil,' said Ludd, pointing to a replica Louis XVI chair lying on its side on the floor. 'Hello, what's this?'

On a small side-table near the overturned chair there was a sheet of paper covered with handwriting. Ludd's eyes widened as he read what was written on the sheet of paper.

'Well I'll be blowed…it's a suicide note,' he said. 'And what's more, it's a confession.'

'A confession to what?' asked Shaw.

'To the murder of Joan Hexham!'

'Severe asphyxiation,' said Dr Holt, the village physician, who had hurried over from his surgery following McPherson's telephone call. 'And probably considerable damage to the larynx as well.'

'But he will live?' asked Shaw, as they stood around Weekes' body lying prostrate on the sofa.

'Hard to say,' murmured the doctor. 'He's in a bad way and ought to be in the cottage hospital. With your permission, Chief Inspector?'

'What?' asked Ludd, who was absorbed in reading the suicide note that Weekes had left on the table. 'Yes, yes – but can he talk?'

'Highly unlikely,' said the doctor. 'There may well be permanent damage to his throat.'

'He can still write though, sir,' observed McPherson. 'Maybe we can…'

'The man is semi-conscious and will not be in a fit state

to be interviewed for some time,' warned Holt. 'Now if I may, I should like to telephone to the cottage hospital to bring the ambulance. He is too unwell to go in my car.'

'Very well,' sighed Ludd. While Holt was telephoning, Ludd called in PC Arbon, who was keeping sentry duty at the front door.

'You go along with Weekes to the cottage hospital,' he told the constable. 'As soon as he wakes up, or says anything – anything at all – I want to know. And don't let him out of your sight – he may be half-dead but he's just confessed to a murder.'

Half an hour later, Weekes had been packed off to the cottage hospital with Dr Holt and PC Arbon in attendance. Ludd rubbed his eyes and sat down on the sofa.

'Proper old caper this has turned out to be,' he said. 'There's me charging Havering with the murder, when all along it was this man Weekes. I've got some explaining to do to Havering.'

'I would'nae worry too much about him,' said McPherson dismissively. 'He's already in trouble over that other charge. He's in no position to cause any fuss.'

'I suppose you're right,' said Ludd. 'And the Scotland Yard chaps have taken that case off our hands, so that's one less thing to worry about. Thank God this happened before the inquest, or I'd look an absolute B.F.'

'Forgive me, Chief Inspector, but may I see the note?' asked Shaw.

'Don't see why not,' said Ludd, and handed it to him.

Shaw read it aloud.

'"I cannot go on living a lie. Whoever finds this will doubtless know who – or what – I am. Joan Hexham threatened to tell others, and I stopped her the only way I could – by stabbing her to death in a moment of madness. Her husband saw me, but I threatened his life to keep him quiet. I pinned the blame on poor Havering, by substituting his knife. But the guilt is too much for me, and I must end it all." Signed, Clarence Weekes.'

'A bit melodramatic, but it explains everything,' said Ludd shaking his head. 'I don't understand it. If he was wracked with guilt, why didn't he just confess to us? He would have had a clean conscience then and the hangman would have done a proper job. He'll have to go through all that again now anyway, the poor devil.'

'Assuming he recovers,' said Shaw.

'Maybe he just couldn't face the thought of a trial,' said McPherson. 'All the sordid details of his life coming out.'

'May I ask,' said Shaw, 'what "details" you are referring to? It seems Mr Weekes had some sort of secret, from what the note says.'

'Mr Weekes,' said Ludd slowly, 'was one of *them*.'

'One of them, er, those, what?' asked Shaw.

Ludd sighed. 'An "unspeakable", Mr Shaw. Of the Oscar Wilde persuasion.'

Shaw raised an eyebrow. 'Ah.'

'Yes,' continued Ludd. 'I did a bit of digging on our Mr Weekes at Police Central Records, as I wondered if there was anything in his past that Mrs Hexham might have found out to blackmail him over. I didn't believe his story about not getting a letter, quite frankly, and it turns out I was probably right. He did have a "past" and I'll bet Joan Hexham found out.'

'What did he do?' asked Shaw.

'Well now...' He cleared his throat and continued. 'He was bound over to keep the peace after attempting to...ah...after attempting to consort with a gentleman in a public convenience, who turned out to be a policeman in plain clothes. It made a few lines in the London evening papers but that was all. Seems that after that he decided to up sticks and move out here where nobody knew him.'

'And so he killed Mrs Hexham to keep her quiet,' said McPherson, 'but then he must have realised his past would come out in Havering's trial and he could'nae face the thought of it.'

'But he surely would have known that would happen,' mused Shaw.

'I thought that, but look at this bit here,' said Ludd, taking the letter from Shaw. Says he stabbed her in a "moment of madness". He wasn't thinking straight.'

'But he must have planned it,' said Shaw. 'He had to substitute Havering's knife, and then carry a knife of his own.'

'A moment of madness can last some time, in my experience,' said Ludd. 'Doesn't mean it happened in a flash. A couple of hours was all it took, when he wasn't thinking straight from fear and anger. I've seen it happen before. And he had a knife anyway, didn't he, it was part of his costume he was wearing on the night of the murder. What a fool I was not to check that.'

'His costume was bloodstained,' added Shaw, 'but of course we assumed that occurred as a result of Havering stabbing Mrs Hexham through the curtain.'

'You had no way of knowing, sir,' said McPherson.

'It's kind of you but don't try to butter me up,' said Ludd. 'I wasn't paying attention to details. Must be getting old.'

'We'd better go over and see what Hexham has to say,' said McPherson. 'Find out if it's true about Weekes threatening him.'

'Blow me, I'd forgotten all about him,' said Ludd. 'What did he have to go and lie to us for? If he'd spoken up about Weekes we could have had this business cleaned up in no time. Come on then. You too Mr Shaw.'

'Ought I to, Chief Inspector? After all, I...'

'Come along Mr Shaw,' said Ludd. 'In for a penny, in for a pound. This'll be our last call of the night anyway so you might as well be there. You seem to have done more work on this case than I have.'

'He's been in there ever since I got here near on an hour ago, sir,' said Special Constable Tanner. 'I seen him through the window, like, because he hasn't drawn the curtains proper in his front room.'

Ludd, McPherson and Shaw stood in the lane opposite Hexham's house, under the shadow of an old pine tree in a neighbouring garden, where Tanner had posted himself on observation duties.

'All right constable,' said Ludd. 'You can get back to your lambs now. Well done.'

'Very good sir,' said Tanner, touching the peak of his cloth cap; he then jogged off along the lane in the direction of Top Farm.

'I'd've torn a strip off him,' murmured McPherson. 'Hadn't even bothered to put his uniform on.'

'He's an off-duty volunteer,' said Ludd. 'I tear a strip off him and he might decide he'd rather join the local darts club than bother to help keep the peace.'

'Aye, but these yokel coppers sir, they're not much better than civilians...'

'"The police are the people and the people are the police",' quoted Ludd. 'That's what Sir Robert Peel said. We're all civilians, and don't you forget it.'

'Well, all right sir...' mumbled McPherson.

'Now,' said Ludd, 'let's see about our Mr Hexham.'

Ludd led the way across the muddy lane to the house opposite.

'I apologise for the intrusion sir,' said Ludd, after Hexham had opened the door. 'May we come in?'

'Of course, Chief Inspector…Flood, isn't it?'

'Ludd.'

'Ah yes. And the vicar too.'

'Reverend Shaw is here on a parish matter,' said Ludd. 'I trust you won't object to him sitting in again?'

'Not at all,' said Hexham. 'Please come in.'

They were shown into the small front parlour which Shaw noticed had now been considerably tidied; there were no piles of paperwork now on display.

'We're here for two reasons, Mr Hexham,' said Ludd. 'The first concerns Mr Shaw as well. I heard from the police doctor today that the post-mortem on your wife has been completed, and therefore arrangements for burial can be made.'

'That's a relief,' said Hexham. 'She needs to be laid to rest.'

'The other matter is rather more serious I'm afraid,' continued Ludd. 'Why did you lie to us about not being able to see anything behind the curtain on stage when your wife was killed?'

'Lied….?' began Hexham.

'Come along now sir,' said Ludd. 'We know from experiments conducted by…ourselves…that there was sufficient light to see what went on behind that curtain. So why did you say you couldn't see anything?'

'I….' Hexham swallowed and his eyes darted from Ludd to McPherson and to Shaw, then back to Ludd. 'I said it because I had no choice.'

'No choice?' asked Ludd.

'Yes,' said Hexham. 'He made me do it. Forced me.'

'He? Who's he?' asked McPherson.

Hexham now stared, looking like the proverbial rabbit with his eyes caught in a motor car's headlamps.

'Mr Weekes,' he said finally. 'Said he'd kill me if I told what I'd saw. Just like that he did, like he was passing the time of day. Whispered it behind that curtain. "Keep quiet," he said, "or this will happen to you as well. Tell them it was dark and neither of us saw anything."'

'Can I make sure I've got this right?' asked Ludd. 'Weekes threatened to kill you? Now why would he do that?'

Hexham's eyes darted around the room again; he swallowed and then finally spoke. 'Because it was him that killed my wife.'

'But Ronald Havering's been charged with your wife's murder, Mr Hexham,' said Ludd slowly. 'Are you telling me that he didn't do it?'

'Havering stabbed her all right,' said Hexham, 'I saw that much behind the curtain. But he can't have killed her. It was just a flesh wound, the knife barely went in. But just after he did that, Weekes took out a knife...and...and...he stabbed her. In the same place. That must have been what killed her.'

'Why on earth didn't you mention this to us?' asked Ludd.

'I couldn't!' blurted Hexham. 'The man had just killed my wife and then threatened to kill *me*. I...I suppose it was the shock. He must be a lunatic. I just went along with what he demanded.'

'It's a very serious matter, Mr Hexham, lying to the police,' said Ludd. 'Under the circumstances however I'm prepared to overlook it.'

'What...what will you do with Weekes?' asked Hexham nervously. 'If he knows I spoke up he'll come here and...'

'Mr Weekes isn't going anywhere,' interrupted Ludd. 'He hanged himself earlier this evening.'

'That's *terrible*,' said Hexham. 'But I can't pretend I'm upset about it, after all, he did kill my wife and would have killed me as well. It's a relief in a way,' he added. 'If he's dead he can't come after me, can he?'

'I didn't say he was dead, Mr Havering,' said Ludd. 'I said he hanged himself. He didn't manage to do the job properly, however, and is still alive.'

'Alive? But he can't…he can't come after me, can he? I mean, the police will have to arrest him, after what I've told you about what he did.'

'He's under police guard in the cottage hospital,' said Ludd. 'I put that in place as a precaution in case he tries to make a run for it.'

'A…run for it?' asked Hexham.

'He's just confessed to the murder of your wife, sir,' said Ludd. 'Put it in a signed letter, he did, the whole story, including threatening you to keep you quiet. So we'll be keeping a close eye on him in case he recovers.'

'In case…?' asked Hexham. 'You mean he might not live?'

'Doctor says he was seconds away from death when we got to him,' said Ludd. 'His throat and lungs and what not are in a terrible state. The slightest obstruction to his airways could finish him off, apparently. We don't want him trying to take the easy way out again, do we?'

'No, no, we don't,' said Hexham angrily. 'If he's to hang, it needs to be legal, with a sentence from a judge. He won't scare me off this time, Chief Inspector. I'll be the first up in that witness box when the time comes, you mark my words.'

'I'm very glad to hear it sir,' said Ludd.

'You'll know about his conviction,' said Hexham.

'Oh, what was that?' asked Ludd airily.

'Well...' said Hexham, hesitating, 'I don't really like to say in front of a vicar, but...'

'Anything you have to say can be said in front of Mr Shaw,' replied Ludd briskly. 'He's what you might call my pastoral advisor in this case.'

'Very well then,' said Hexham. 'Weekes was a degenerate. Convicted of – I won't dignify it with a name but...I'm not saying his kind would be more likely to commit murder, but, well, he's not exactly a paragon of virtue, is what I'm saying.'

'We know about Weekes' inclinations,' said Ludd. 'He paid his dues for that and it's over and done with. What I'd like to know is how *you* know about it.'

'That was my wife,' said Hexham proudly. 'Found out all sorts of things from the London Newspaper Library and Cuttings Agency, she did. Enquiries answered promptly by post for a fee.'

'And why did she do that?' asked McPherson. 'What business of hers was it?'

'Well, she had to know who she was inviting on to the committee,' said Hexham defensively. 'We were founder members you know. Of the Lower Addenham Dramatic Society. The handling of money was involved, as well as the supervision of minors. We couldn't just let anyone sit on the committee without knowing if they had something in their past we ought to have been aware of. You'll find the same thing's done in any respectable voluntary organisation.'

'Maybe so,' said McPherson, 'but they don't then start blackmailing people over what they've found.'

'That's a very nasty word Sergeant,' said Hexham, 'and I'll thank you not to use it in reference to my late wife.'

'Or what?' said McPherson. 'Ye can't slander the dead.'

'All right, sergeant, thank you,' said Ludd. 'If you don't call it blackmail, what do you call it, Mr Hexham?' he added.

Hexham sniffed and clutched the lapels of his waistcoat like a barrister in court. 'My wife merely sent letters advising potential committee members that she was aware of…certain questionable activities in their pasts, and that she would be keeping an eye on them to make sure that they behaved themselves in accordance with the high moral principles expected of those using premises under the administration of the Church of England.'

'But the village hall is only nominally linked to the church,' said Shaw. 'Yours is a secular organisation. I do not see that you had any right to enquire into the histories of your volunteers.'

'On that point we must differ,' sniffed Hexham. 'Society is drifting in a very immoral direction, if you ask me, and perhaps if the Church took more interest in…'

'Yes, yes, all right thank you,' interrupted Ludd. 'We'll save the subject of the moral decline of the nation for another time. Did you actually see any of the letters your wife sent regarding the…morality…of the committee members?'

'Ah…no,' said Hexham after a pause. 'She only mentioned briefly what she had found out.'

'I see,' said Ludd. 'Well, we won't take up any more of your time sir.' He made to leave the room.

'Is…is that all then?' asked Hexham. 'You're sure Weekes isn't going to come after me?'

'Mr Weekes will be lucky if he has the strength to open his eyes, any time in the foreseeable future,' said Ludd. 'You needn't worry about him.'

Once outside on the village high street, Ludd and McPherson stopped outside the village police house, whilst Shaw made to walk up the hill back to the vicarage.

'Poor devil,' said Ludd, shaking his head.

'Who?' enquired McPherson.

'Hexham,' replied Ludd. 'Thinks him and his wife are paragons of virtue when he's got no idea how nasty those letters were.'

'Aye,' said McPherson. 'It'll come out in court, though. He ought to be told before then.'

'Hmm, perhaps you're right,' said Ludd. 'Mr Shaw, I wonder if you would be good enough at some point over the next few days to have another word with Hexham and perhaps prepare him for the inevitable character assassination of his wife that will happen at the trial?'

'Of course,' said Shaw.

'Assuming of course, there is a trial. Let's hope Weekes doesn't avoid judgement by shuffling off his mortal coil before then.'

Shaw felt it was not the right time to point out that Ludd had quoted *Hamlet* again.

'None of us can avoid our ultimate judgement, Chief Inspector,' said Shaw.

Ludd coughed, appearing embarrassed. 'Yes, well, that's us done then, he said, extending his hand to Shaw. 'Thanks for all your help, sir. Just a few loose ends to tie up but that's the case pretty much closed. Goodnight.'

'Goodnight, Chief Inspector, and Detective Sergeant,' said Shaw, as the two men disappeared into the rural gloom. He walked home, deep in thought.

'A most peculiar person left a telephone message for you,' said Shaw's wife when he arrived home. 'Hettie took it, and said she could barely hear a word he said. Something about the Duke of Norfolk. I don't understand, is it a house party of some sort?'

Shaw looked at the name and number on the message pad by the telephone, and chuckled. 'I suspect the only house involved is the public one named the "Duke of Norfolk", opposite the cathedral in Midchester.'

'Oh,' said Mrs Shaw. 'Why on earth are men in public houses calling you on the telephone?'

'A journalist,' said Shaw. 'Normally I dislike speaking to them, but this one may be of considerable help in the murder case.'

'I shall leave you to it,' said Mrs Shaw. 'I'd rather not get involved with your amateur detective work. I'm sure you ought to leave it to Chief Inspector Ludd. Your supper, by the way, is cold, and waiting on the dining room table.'

Mrs Shaw went into the drawing room, and Shaw sensed she was unhappy that he had missed his evening meal, but rather than go in straight away he decided he ought to first telephone to the public house.

There was a terrific din on the line and at first he thought he had been connected to some sort of factory or workshop, but at last he was able to make himself heard and was connected by a harassed-sounding man to the journalist.

'Mr Gutteridge?' asked Shaw.

'Ah, vicar,' said the reporter. He sounded, thought Shaw, as if an evening of serious drinking was already well underway. 'Thank you for calling back. I've some news for you. About those names you wanted me to investigate.'

'Would you be kind enough to send the cuttings in the post to me?' asked Shaw.

'Already done it, by the last post,' said Gutteridge proudly. 'Copied 'em out by hand. You'll get it tomorrow. You've some sorts in your village, I'll say that much.'

'Sorts?'

'Yes, that Weekes, for example, he was had up for...'

'I know about Mr Weekes.'

'Ah well then. And that Madame Dubois. Cor!'

Shaw's curiosity got the better of him. 'Would you give me a brief summary of what you found out about Madame Dubois?'

Shaw raised an eyebrow as Gutteridge outlined what he had discovered.

'You have been most helpful, Mr Gutteridge,' he said, after the man had finished speaking.

'I'm not doing it out of kindness, Mr Shaw,' said Gutteridge. 'We made a bargain, if you remember. An exclusive interview with you in return for the information.'

'Indeed I do remember,' said Shaw, 'and if you call at the vicarage at your earliest convenience I shall be pleased to speak to you.'

'Ah, that's good of you vicar, but, well, look here. The deadline for tomorrow's *Morning Chronicle* – that's our sister paper – is in an hour and it would be good if you could give me something to put in it. A titbit, like. '

Shaw thought for a moment, listening to the hubbub of public house conversation and the staccato sound of a player-piano in the background.

'Very well, Mr Gutteridge,' he said. 'There is one "titbit" I can give you about the murder case, on condition that my name is not mentioned.'

'Right you are, vicar.'

'Do you have pencil and paper?'

'Always do.'

'Very well. Then listen carefully.'

Chapter Ten

The following morning Shaw read the daily service of Morning Prayer as usual in the village church, conscious that he was rushing through it somewhat; fortunately, as was usually the case, only the verger was present. He decided to be brisk, but not hurried; after all, the work he was carrying out might not fall within the accepted duties of a clergyman, but it was, he concluded, of the utmost importance.

After the service was ended, he hurried back to the vicarage and was pleased to see that the morning post had arrived. Hettie was just about to pick it up but with a hasty 'pardon me,' he stooped to pick up a large brown foolscap envelope, which he took into his study, opening it with his little finger as he went.

As he had hoped, it was from Fred Gutteridge, who had managed to catch the night post; the journalist had summarised the press articles he had managed to find on the names that Shaw had given him. Dubois, Weekes and Hexham. He had not bothered to ask for any information on Cranston or Havering, as he already knew the subject of their blackmail letters from what Chief Inspector Ludd had told him.

Weekes' transgression he had since learned of also, and he put those notes aside. The name of Hexham had been found in a small article in a county newspaper some months ago; police had investigated a series of financial irregularities in his chain of shops, but had been unable to come to any satisfactory conclusion. The name had also appeared in a small announcement in the *East Anglian Daily Times* from the previous year: a Josiah Barrow Esquire of Overview Farm near King's Lynn, Norfolk, much loved, pillar of the Baptist Chapel *etcetera etcetera* had gone to his reward and left the entirety of his fortune to his only daughter, one Joan Hexham of Lower Addenham, Suffolk.

Interesting, thought Shaw, but of little significance in comparison to the summary of an article on Madame Dubois, taken from a national Sunday newspaper of dubious reputation.

It seemed that when she had married her husband, one Charles Haskins, it had caused something of a stir in society circles and her past had been investigated. She had worked as a waitress in her father's café – a bad enough crime in itself in the eyes of snobbish English society – but there was worse to come.

The café had been a popular haunt of German soldiers, and there was a rumour that the eighteen-year old had been, for a short time, the mistress of a high-ranking German officer. 'Romantically linked,' the article said primly, but it was clear what the implication was. For this, Madame Dubois, or *madamoiselle* as she was then – had been given a nickname by her neighbours: *La Traîtresse*.

The traitor.

Shaw, deep in thought, suddenly looked up as he heard a loud knocking on the study door. 'Come in,' he said.

It was Mrs Shaw, and she carried in her hand a newspaper which she placed, rather forcefully, on Shaw's desk.

'I think you ought to see this,' she said.

It was a copy of the *Midchester Morning Chronicle.*

'It was delivered while you were out at church,' she continued, 'and I am sorry to say that Hettie has already seen it, in fact it was she who remarked upon it. Look at the front page.'

Shaw looked at the headline: 'Addenham Murder: Shocking Revelations. By Reginald Gutteridge'.

He scanned the article; it was much as he had expected, breaking the news that Weekes had confessed to the murder of Mrs Hexham and then tried to hang himself; and that consequently, charges against Havering would have to be dropped.

'What of it?' asked Shaw. 'I mentioned this to you last night after supper, if you recall.'

'I'm not referring to the main article. Look at the one next to it,' said Mrs Shaw.

In a little box next to the main feature was a smaller article in bold type with the heading 'The Cross and the Truncheon: how a village cleric is beating the police at their own game.'

'"Sin simmers below the surface of the quiet Suffolk village where three murders have taken place in recent years,"' read Shaw out loud. 'Oh dear, Mr Gutteridge has rather gone off into flights of fantasy.'

'Carry on reading,' said Mrs Shaw. 'There's something about you there which I think you ought to see.'

Shaw read on, and then slammed his fist in anger on the desk. Mrs Shaw jumped slightly.

'I'm sorry, my dear,' said Shaw. 'Leave this with me. I shall telephone the writer and demand a retraction.'

He got up and walked briskly to the telephone in the hallway, and asked for a Midchester number.

A few moments later he was put through, and asked to speak to Fred Gutteridge.

After a pause he was connected to a prim-sounding telephonist in a noisy room; he was certain that he heard Gutteridge call out something indistinct and then laugh.

'I'm sorry sir, Mr Gutteridge is not available at this time,' she said. 'Would you kindly call back later?'

'Quite frankly, young lady,' said Shaw with some irritation, 'I do not believe you. Kindly connect me right away.'

'Mr Gutteridge is *not* available,' said the woman in a less polite tone this time. 'Would you care to leave a message?'

'No I would not, madam,' said Shaw. 'The only message I wish you to relay is that I intend to remain on this line until I am connected with Mr Gutteridge, and to Hades with the expense! I am sure he does not wish other important calls to be blocked.'

There was a sigh, and then the line clicked off; Shaw thought he had been disconnected but then he heard Gutteridge's jovial voice.

'Vicar! Good morning to you sir! What can I do for you?'

'Good morning, Mr Gutteridge,' said Shaw. 'I shall be brief. I made it quite clear that my name was not to be mentioned in connection with the information I gave you over the telephone last night, and yet you have printed an article which mentions me several times.'

'Come on now, vicar,' wheedled Gutteridge. 'It doesn't say it was you that gave me the tip off, now does it? Just a bit of background on your sleuthing, like.'

'It is full of half-truths and gossip,' said Shaw.

Gutteridge chuckled. 'That's most newspaper articles. Anything in particular you object to?'

'This sentence for a start,' said Shaw. '"Reverend Shaw tucks another case under his cassock, notching up three-nil against the Suffolk Constabulary in recent high profile murder cases. This newspaper asks why Chief Inspector

Ludd of the Midchester CID has his work done for him by a parson."'

'Well, that's true, isn't it?' exclaimed Gutteridge.

'Certainly not,' said Shaw. 'I have never "beaten the police at their own game" and nor do I intend to.'

'Anything else?'

'Yes,' said Shaw. 'There some disgraceful nonsense about myself also. This line for example. "Reverend Shaw, tall, dark and handsome" – the first item is the only correct one, the second manifestly untrue as you have seen me with my hat off, and the third purely subjective. But it is this sentence to which I particularly object. "The vicar is popular with the village womenfolk, and is known to have recently attended a gathering of several attractive young ladies in the village hall, some of them visibly pregnant." That, I presume, was my recent address to the Mother's Union!'

'All right, all right vicar,' said Gutteridge. 'Maybe I did get a bit carried away. I'd had four pints when I wrote that and perhaps I was feeling a bit too jovial. Nothing I can do about it now.'

'I beg to differ,' said Shaw. 'I insist that you print a correction in tomorrow's edition stating that I have never attempted to subvert the activities of the Criminal Investigation Department.'

'Now look here, Mr Shaw, I can't just…'

'Do you or do you not want the full "exclusive" that we discussed previously?'

'You can't just back out on that, vicar, we had a deal.'

'I am not backing out on anything. In your profession it has perhaps been forgotten that the word of a gentleman is his bond. It is you who have jeopardised the agreement by printing scurrilous gossip. A simple one-line retraction will suffice, and I will then be pleased to confer with you on a *truthful* article.'

'Oh, all right then,' grumbled Gutteridge. 'Have it your own way. But I hope it's worth it as I spent a good long time in that newspaper library for you. Got the notes, did you?'

'Yes, thank you,' said Shaw. 'They were most enlightening. Good day to you.'

Just as Shaw replaced the telephone receiver there was the sound of the bell-pull from the front door nearby.

'It is quite all right, Hettie, I shall go,' he called as the servant emerged from the back kitchen.

After his successful confrontation with Gutteridge he felt inspired to give a piece of his mind to any other journalists who wished to distort the truth; he felt sure that this caller would be part of the inevitable gang of reporters that would now descend on the village again given the news of Weekes' confession.

Instead he was surprised to see Chief Inspector Ludd on the doorstep. The policeman raised his hat and bid the vicar good morning.

'Oh ho,' he said, pointing at the newspaper in Shaw's hand. 'Read all the nonsense they've written about you, have you?'

'Unfortunately yes,' said Shaw. 'I have also demanded a full retraction, which Mr Gutteridge has promised.'

'I wouldn't wager much on that happening,' said Ludd. 'What I'd like to know is who the devil told him about Weekes? It's not in any of the other papers. My guess is it was someone at the cottage hospital who overheard something. Now if I get the time I'll pay this Mr Gutteridge a...'

'On that subject,' interrupted Shaw, trying not to sound overly guilty, 'I ought to tell you something. Won't you come in?'

'I haven't really got time just now thank you sir,' said Ludd. 'I'm only here to tie up a few loose ends and then I'm due in court, so I won't stay. Oh, by the way, you might like to know that we had a look around Weekes' cottage earlier, and we found a blackmail letter amongst his things. Handwriting matches the other ones, so it seems Mrs Hexham knew all about what he got up to in his private life, poor devil. Anyway, that's by-the-by. I just came to deliver this.'

He passed an envelope to Shaw.

'I said I'd wait for a reply,' he added.

Shaw opened the envelope; inside was a note written in a painstakingly neat feminine hand. He read it to himself.

'Mr and Mrs George Ludd request the pleasure of your company at a supper party to be held at "The Laurels", 174, Hazeldene Avenue, Nr Midchester, Suffolk.' Today's date followed, and below that in smaller letters in the corner was added 'Lounge suits.'

'A small occasion to celebrate closing the investigation,' said Ludd proudly. 'McPherson and his wife will be there too. A sort of thank you for your help, as well.'

'My help?' asked Shaw.

'Yes, in that business with Havering. If it weren't for you I doubt that girl would have come forward.'

'Ah,' said Shaw. 'A sad business. But yes, you can tell Mrs Ludd I shall be pleased to attend. Mrs Shaw no doubt will come also if she is free this evening.'

'That's all right then,' said Ludd, breathing out. 'We weren't sure of the, what do you call it, etiquette for this sort of thing, but Mrs Ludd looked it up in a book, so I hope the invite was done properly.'

'Most satisfactorily,' said Shaw. 'I believe your nearest station is Midchester North?'

'No need for trains, Mr Shaw,' said Ludd proudly. 'I'll

collect you and the lady wife in my motor car after I've finished with Arbon at the police house this evening. I'll drop you back home as well, so there's no need to worry about that. Shall we say seven pm? We usually have our tea earlier, but Mrs Ludd said 7.30 was the proper time for a smart do.'

'That will be acceptable,' said Shaw. 'By the way, is there any news of Mr Weekes?'

'I telephoned to the hospital this morning,' said Ludd, 'and Arbon says there's not much change. Still touch and go, although he's been muttering and whispering apparently. Mentioned Hexham, and Madame Dubois, but it was only their names Arbon could make out.'

'I see, thank you,' said Shaw. 'Until this evening, then.' As he closed the front door, he thought of Mrs Hexham, en route to some dreary municipal cemetery; Weekes lying in hospital with nothing ahead but death on the gallows, and Gladys Kersey languishing in prison, and wondered if there was much at all to celebrate.

Later that day Shaw was putting the final touches to his sermon for Ash Wednesday. As he sat at his desk in the little study, with Fraser asleep at his feet and the little fire glowing (Hettie had the frugal ability to keep a fire burning with what seemed like nothing more than three pieces of coal and a twist of newspaper), his mind began to wander.

It all seemed obvious; Weekes had confessed to the murder of Mrs Hexham, and there was nothing more for Shaw to do other than stand and wait to be called as a witness in the forthcoming trial. But then, he thought, it had 'all seemed obvious' when Havering had been charged with the killing.

Something was not right, but at present, that 'something' presented itself in his mind as disjointed and disconnected images. The village hall...a man walking along the high street at night...what did it all mean?

Quickly he thumbed through his prayer book until he found what he was looking for, and knelt at the little baroque-style *prie-dieu* in the corner of the room. His wife disliked it, saying it looked like the sort of thing a French countess would have in her bedroom, but he found it helped focus his attention more than simply praying while seated at his desk.

He murmured under his breath one of the prayers for Morning Prayer which he normally overlooked, but which now seemed appropriate.

'"Almighty God, the fountain of all wisdom, who knowest our necessities before we ask, and our ignorance in asking: We beseech thee to have compassion upon our infirmities; and those things, which for our unworthiness we dare not, and for our blindness we cannot ask, vouchsafe to give us for the worthiness of thy Son Jesus Christ our Lord. Amen."'

He got up and returned to his desk and reached for his pipe and tobacco pouch. He did not feel particularly enlightened after the prayer, but there was a sense of the disconnected images in his mind coming more into focus, like pictures in a magic-lantern display. He scooped his pipe into the leather pouch and frowned as it yielded only a few tiny flakes. Looking to the glass jar on the chimney-piece, he saw that was empty too. He realised he had been smoking more than usual; something that often happened when he was wrestling with a mental puzzle.

'Come on Fraser,' he said to his dog. 'A quick walk to

the stores will do us good.'

Fraser leapt to his feet; it never ceased to amuse Shaw how the animal was able to go from deep sleep to frenetic activity in less than a heartbeat.

A few minutes later they were in the cosy, cluttered surroundings of the village stores. Shaw kept Fraser on a tight lead lest the dog should start investigating some of the products near the floor too closely.

'Morning vicar,' said Cranston, as he emerged from the back room. 'What can I do for you?'

'Two ounces of Three Nuns, please,' said Shaw.

'Right you are sir,' said Cranston, and began scooping tobacco from a large jar onto a scale on the counter.

'Was that you I saw on the way down the high street last night, vicar?' asked Cranston cautiously. 'Only I wasn't sure, like, so apologies for not saying hello.'

Shaw jumped slightly. He had been hoping to broach this subject and was not prepared for it to have come up so quickly.

'Ah, yes,' said Shaw. 'That was me. I also was not sure if it was you, hence I did not greet you.'

'Quite all right,' said Cranston amiably. 'Gets pitch black down there of an evening this time of year,' he added.

'You were...out for some shooting, I take it?' asked Shaw. You appeared to be carrying a shotgun bag.'

'Ah, that wasn't no shotgun,' said Cranston. 'It was this.' He reached under the counter and produced a slim, lightweight rifle. 'I keep it in a bag when I'm out, as between you and me I haven't a certificate for it.'

'A point two-two, I think?' asked Shaw. 'For birds?'

'Not this time, vicar,' said Cranston. 'That's for rats, that is. If you got a problem with rats in a storeroom, like we have sometimes, it's the best thing. Traps and poison is no good. We got a cat, but the rats is too big for him and he's scared of 'em. And a shotgun would cause more damage to my stock than those blasted rats ever would. This'll kill a man at close range, so it makes short work of a rat. Best thing for 'em.'

'Apart from one of these,' said Shaw, pointing to Fraser.

'A terrier's well and good,' replied Cranston, 'and I had one brought in once, but we can't keep one because of our cat. He's the wife's little friend now. Here boy,' he said leaning down to pet Fraser.

Fraser gave a low growl and bared his teeth.

'Doesn't seem to like me much,' chuckled Cranston. 'Must be the smell of our cat on me.'

'Do you have another store outside the village?' asked Shaw.

'Another store?' said Cranston, as he weighed the tobacco and shovelled it into a paper bag, 'no, I don't. It wasn't me using the rifle last night if that's what you mean. I was only collecting it. I lent it to Mr Hexham down the road. His store over at Midchester's rife with rats. He came in asking for poison and I told him "this gun's better than any poison and I'll charge you less for the use of it. Paid me five bob, he did, including ammunition, but he never discharged it. Said the little bast...blighters was hiding from him.'

'I see,' said Shaw. 'I shall bear the information in mind should we have any such problems at the vicarage. Fortunately Fraser is a good ratter.'

'That's two and tuppence ha'penny, sir,' said Cranston, handing over the tobacco. 'I'll put that on your account as I know you're a prompt payer.'

Shaw disliked the way most men of his class put off paying tradesmen's bills until the very last moment. Instead he always paid on time; a habit which ensured him good service with the local shopkeepers.

'Anything else?' asked Cranston.

'No thank you,' said Shaw, and turned to go.

'Oh, vicar,' said Cranston lightly. 'Heard anything about our Mr Weekes? I saw all about you finding him, in the paper today.'

Shaw paused at the door. 'It was myself and the police. He is still in a very poor way, I understand,' he said. 'He could die at any moment.'

'Well, maybe that would be for the best,' said Cranston. 'If he's going to hang anyway, it would have saved everyone a lot of bother if he'd only been discovered a bit later.'

Shaw said nothing other than 'good day,' and left the shop. The blurred images in his mind had suddenly fallen into sharp focus.

The bell of Madame Dubois' shop jingled merrily as Shaw pushed the door open. The proprietress sat at the counter, reading a newspaper with a listless expression on her face, which changed to a welcoming smile as she recognised the vicar.

'Ah, Mr Shaw,' she said brightly. 'I read of you in the newspaper. How clever you must be to help the police in these matters.'

'I assure you my role was very slight in the recent events,' said Shaw. 'The journalist got rather carried away.'

'Perhaps,' said Madame Dubois. 'Is there any news of Mr Weekes? I am happy that the killer has been found, but I read in the newspaper he tried commit the suicide, without success.'

'That is the reason for my call,' said Shaw. 'Mr Weekes is

in a very bad way. The doctors are not sure he will survive.'

'*Quel dommage,*' said Madame Dubois. 'But he will surely go to the *guillotine*, I mean, the hanging place, now that he has confessed? It may be a blessing for him to die soon instead.'

'That is highly likely, from what I have been told,' said Shaw. 'And that is why I have come to you. Mr Weekes has mentioned your name. It may be of help if you would visit him in hospital.'

'Me? But why should I talk to him, the man is a killer.'

'It may aid his recovery if he were to see a friendly face. The only other person he has mentioned is Mr Hexham, and it would hardly be appropriate for them to meet, I fear.'

'But what would it achieve to see him?' asked Madame Dubois. 'If the man is dying, he will not last much longer.'

'It may be of use in the case,' said Shaw. 'If you were to corroborate his confession, it would be of great help. He may wish to confide in a friend, rather than the police. '

'He is not really a friend,' protested Madame Dubois, 'and it says in this newspaper he is always under the police guard in hospital. Surely, that means he is most dangerous.'

'It is more to protect him, Madame Dubois, from harming himself any further. But, of course, we live in a wicked world and there are ghoulish people from the newspapers who will wish to photograph him and so on. Mr Weekes is in a ground floor room with French doors facing the lawn; it is rather a vulnerable situation and the Chief Inspector felt it best for him to be under constant guard.'

'I would feel uncomfortable sitting there with some policeman looking at me,' said Madame Dubois. 'And I do not think Mr Weekes will confess to anything if one is looking at *him*.'

'No doubt Constable Arbon will leave you in peace for a short while if I ask him,' said Shaw. 'Please come.'

'Very well,' said Madame Dubois after a pause. 'When should I go?'

'It is too late today, but nine o'clock tomorrow morning, perhaps? I shall be happy to accompany you to the hospital. I believe you have a motor car.'

'Yes, that is correct,' said Madame Dubois. 'Very well then. Iris can look after the shop. *Jusqu'à demain.* Good day, Mr Shaw.'

It was late evening in the gleaming new mock-Tudor dining room of 'The Laurels', Chief Inspector Ludd's villa on the Midchester bypass.

'Well, what do you think, Mr Shaw? Not a bad place, eh?'

Ludd sat back in his Jacobean style carver-chair, loosened his waistcoat, and lit a cigar which was, Shaw judged by the smell, made of rather cheap tobacco.

Shaw had been brought up to believe it was bad manners to make observations, whether good or ill, about other people's houses, and so merely murmured his assent.

'A very well set-up house,' he said non-committally as he packed his pipe. 'And an excellent meal, thank you.'

Shaw sat to Ludd's right at the dining table, and McPherson was opposite, puffing on a cigarette. It seemed that Mrs Ludd had studied her book of etiquette carefully and had announced after dinner that the ladies would be going into the 'the drawing room lounge' as she called it, for coffee. She had presumably read that it was correct form for the men to be left to their own devices for a while before joining them.

'Don't thank me,' said Ludd expansively, 'thank the wife. She's always been a good cook. That's one reason we don't have a servant; there's no way I'd find a better cook in Christendom than Mrs Ludd.'

'Aye, you're right there,' said McPherson with a sigh.

'Are you settling in well, Sergeant McPherson?' asked Shaw. 'I understand you and your wife are to lodge here for a while.'

'Early days yet but my wife seems happy, which is the main thing,' said McPherson.

'Indeed all the ladies seem to be getting along well,' said Shaw, after a peal of feminine laughter had rung out from the neighbouring room. 'But then, Mrs Shaw is always visiting all sorts and conditions of people, as the wife of a clergyman. She has the knack of fitting in.'

'And it helps to have the Chief Inspector around to speak if I've something on my mind about work,' said McPherson.

'Drop more wine, Mr Shaw?' said Ludd, picking up a bottle from the table. 'That's good stuff, that is. An Empire Burgundy wine, it's called. From South Africa, believe it or not, the man in the vintner's said. And there was me thinking all wines came from France! Only two-and-nine a bottle, well, you can't go wrong can you?'

Shaw accepted another glass, and had to admit to himself it was not a bad wine, and at such a reasonable price he made a mental note to procure a case. He balked when he thought of his claret bill from Berry Brothers and Rudd; he really ought to cut down on that sort of thing, he reflected, in these difficult economic times.

'Well then,' said Ludd lifting his glass, 'here's to a successfully concluded case.'

Shaw raised his glass and took a sip; Ludd and McPherson emptied theirs with relish.

'On that subject, do you not find it wearing to "talk shop" at home?' asked Shaw.

'Not so far, no, I don't think so,' said Ludd. 'But it's only been a day or so. Matter of fact, now that you've mentioned it, there is something that's been puzzling me. About who told that Gutteridge person that Weekes had confessed to the murder. You were about to mention something about that this morning, I think, Mr Shaw.'

'Ah…' replied Shaw. 'It was I that told him.'

There was a moment of silence and the temperature in the room seemed to have dropped, despite the little gas fire glowing merrily in the grate.

'Now look here, Mr Shaw,' said Ludd, with a face like thunder. 'I've been happy to consult with you on this case, and even invite you into my home, because I thought I could trust you. But it seems now I can't.'

Shaw raised a hand. 'You have every right to be angry, Chief Inspector. But perhaps, if I might explain…'

The following morning Shaw called at Madame Dubois' house on the edge of the village. Her car, a large, sleek Lanchester saloon, was already on the driveway. A few moments later she was driving it effortlessly along the country lane which led to the little cottage hospital built to serve the villages of Lower Addenham, Addenham Magna and the town of Great Netley.

The hospital, a squat Edwardian building whose rustic

design did not quite hide its institutional origins, hoved into view, and Madame Dubois brought the car to a skidding halt on the gravel drive.

'I have been worrying all night,' she said to Shaw. 'You say that he could die at any moment?'

'Quite so,' said Shaw. 'He is very weak. The slightest obstruction to his airway might be sufficient.'

'*Terrible*,' said Madame Dubois. 'I hope I can be of some use.'

'This way,' said Shaw, assisting the lady to step out of her motor car. He nodded to the commissionaire at the door, and led Madame Dubois down a gleaming clean corridor smelling of antiseptic and fresh linen. One or two invalids in bath-chairs eyed the pair with curiosity; Shaw guessed they knew who he was and who the special patient being kept in the private room at the end of the corridor was also.

Constable Arbon was standing just outside the door of the room; upon seeing the pair arrive he gave a small salute and nod, and ushered them in.

'Morning vicar,' he said. 'Ma'am.'

'Any change?' asked Shaw.

They looked towards the bed; Weekes lay still and appeared to be asleep; his breathing was laboured and heavy. Beside his bed was the door to a small bathroom, and opposite were French doors with a view of the hospital grounds.

'Still touch and go, as they say, sir' said Arbon. 'He's mentioned the lady 'ere a few times though, I know that much.'

'We must hurry,' said Madame Dubois. 'May I be left alone?'

Madame Dubois flashed a smile of such brilliance towards Arbon that she might have been an actress in a

Hollywood film. The constable blushed.

'I don't know about that ma'am...' he stammered.

'It's quite all right, constable,' said Shaw. 'You may have a rest from your duties for a short while. The Chief Inspector has given his approval.'

'That's all right then, sir,' said Arbon. 'I'll have myself a quick cup of tea and a smoke.'

'Very well,' said Shaw. 'And I shall be in the corridor should you need me, Madame Dubois.'

'That is most kind,' said the Belgian woman. 'I shall not be long.'

Shaw and Arbon stepped out of the room. Arbon lit a cigarette, but did not seem interested in finding the cup of tea he had mentioned earlier.

Shaw listened at the door; he heard the low murmur of Madame Dubois' voice, but could not make out the words. There was a brief silence, and then, a loud scream.

Then came a short blast on a police whistle; Shaw flew into action and rammed the door open. He almost collided with Chief Inspector Ludd, who was holding Madame Dubois in a half-Nelson. She was struggling like a madwoman and calling out a string of imprecations in French, only a few of which Shaw understood. McPherson was in front of her shielding Weekes. Shaw noticed a flash of movement at the French doors.

'Constable, that man, quickly!' he called.

Arbon needed no further encouragement and raced across the room. Without pausing to look for a catch or handle, he forced the doors open with his shoulder; the right hand door flew outwards and hit a figure outside, who fell to the ground. Arbon dived on top of the man and in an instant, had secured his arm behind his back.

By now Ludd had gained control of Madame Dubois, and he and McPherson frogmarched her out on to the terrace. Shaw waved into the corridor, and a doctor and nurse quickly entered the room to examine Weekes.

'He's all right,' said the doctor. 'No change.'

Shaw nodded and stepped out onto the terrace, closing the French doors behind him. Arbon had hauled the bewildered-looking man on the terrace to his feet and secured his hands behind his back with handcuffs.

'Helene Dubois,' said Ludd, breathing heavily, 'I am arresting you for conspiring to murder Joan Hexham, and for the attempted murder of Clarence Weekes.'

He then turned to the man who had been found on the patio. 'Reginald Hexham, I am arresting you for the attempted murder of Clarence Weekes on a separate occasion, and for the murder of your wife.'

Chapter Eleven

Several months had passed; spring had come and gone and summer had arrived, and was itself now in its waning days, and the slow wheels of British justice had completed their revolutions.

Reginald Hexham, by means of the hangman's rope, had been summoned to give account of himself – to a Power far higher than that of the Norwich Assizes – for the murder of his wife. Helene Dubois had been spared such a summons for the time being, but was to be detained at Holloway for a term of not less than 20 years for her part in the conspiracy.

Shaw sat in a shaft of sunlight in a quiet corner of the George, sipping at a china mug of mild. Opposite him was Fred Gutteridge, balancing a notebook, pencil, cigarette, beer mug, and whisky shot-glass with practised ease. Next to Gutteridge sat Ludd and McPherson, both with their arms crossed, glowering at the journalist.

'I don't see why the police have to be here,' said Gutteridge. 'I came here to question the Rev.'

'Mr Shaw kindly invited us along to make sure whatever you write tallies with the official police report,' said Ludd. 'So just you mind what you do.'

'I had to wait long enough for it, didn't I?' said Gutteridge to nobody in particular.

'It would not have been possible to discuss the case in

any great detail before the judge had passed sentence,' said Shaw. 'It would have been *sub judice*.'

'That means Mr Shaw was no' allowed to talk about...' began McPherson.

'I know what *sub judice* means,' said Gutteridge wearily. 'Blimey, give me a bit of credit. And anyway, it was supposed to be an exclusive,' complained Gutteridge.

'And so it shall be,' said Shaw. 'An exclusive, I believe, simply means I have not given the story to any other newspaper. It does not entitle you to speak to myself alone, and not hear anybody else's side of the story. This case was conducted by Chief Inspector Ludd with the assistance of Sergeant McPherson. I merely acted in a minor role.'

'Oh, very well then,' said Gutteridge, taking a long sip of beer. 'My editor didn't let me cover the court case on account of it taking place too far away, up in Norwich – he sent a local man instead – so I never got to hear the full details. Hence I might sound a bit behind-hand, so you'll need to explain everything properly.'

'I shall do my best,' said Shaw.

'Right then,' replied Gutteridge. He picked up his pad and licked the end of his pencil.

'What was it that first made you suspicious?' he asked. 'The Chief Inspector here charged Ronald Havering with the murder. Why did you think otherwise?'

'I could not believe,' said Shaw, 'that Havering would deliberately murder Mrs Hexham in so obvious a way, in front of dozens of witnesses. It would have been the act of a madman, and he appeared perfectly sane. It seemed to me that suspicion fell on him largely because of his involvement in a completely separate matter.'

'Ah, that's the other story I'm working on,' said Gutteridge. "The Dirty Doctor and his Den of Debauchery:

an expose of...'

'As I said,' interrupted Shaw quickly, 'that is a separate matter and one which I have no wish to discuss with you. May we continue?'

'Shame,' said Gutteridge. 'All right then, carry on.'

'The first inkling I had that something was not right,' continued Shaw, 'was during the technical rehearsal. Madame Dubois seemed particularly concerned that she should embrace Havering, and yet it was not mentioned in the script. Shakespeare rarely put stage directions in his plays.'

'So?' said Gutteridge. 'These actresses are always doing things like that, aren't they? Adding little bits of their own in to sort of flesh out the character. It's what they do.'

'Yes,' said Shaw, 'but when I spoke to Madame Dubois in her shop some time later, she claimed she had very little knowledge of Shakespeare, which seemed at odds with what she had said during the rehearsal.'

'And that made you suspicious of her?' asked Gutteridge.

'Not at first,' replied Shaw. 'But I began to notice various things which did not seem to tally with the views of Chief Inspector Ludd.'

'I wish you'd mentioned all this before,' murmured the detective.

'Nothing was certain in my mind,' said Shaw, 'and I did not wish to bother you with "half-baked" theories. I needed to be certain.'

'And what made you certain?' asked Gutteridge.

'A culmination of various small things,' said Shaw. 'First, I became suspicious of the activities of Madame Dubois. Hexham claimed his wife's only social activity apart from the amateur theatricals was to attend the ladies' knitting circle at the village hall. Whilst in the hall I noticed a time-table which stated that the circle met on Wednesday afternoons. When I spoke later to Madame Dubois, she claimed that she visited Mrs Hexham at home to practice her lines...'

'Let me guess,' interrupted Gutteridge with a wolfish expression. 'She went round there on Wednesday afternoons.'

'Precisely.'

'So she was actually visiting *Mr* Hexham, not his wife.'

'I fear so,' said Shaw.

'Cor, this is sensational stuff,' said Gutteridge, as he scribbled rapidly on his notepad. 'They never mentioned much of this in the official court report. Go on. Any more details of the love affair?'

'Certainly not,' said Shaw. 'Suffice to say, it made me question just how genuine Hexham's apparent grief was over his wife's death. I became more suspicious after seeing the very interesting information that you unearthed from your newspaper library.'

'Ah,' replied Gutteridge. 'That's all the stuff about Madame carrying on with a high-up Hun during the war, isn't it? Yes, I'll have to work that in to the article somehow.'

'If you please,' said Shaw, raising his hand, 'I would prefer that you report only the salient details.'

'This was about her being nicknamed "the traitor" over in Belgium, wasn't it, Mr Shaw?' asked Ludd. 'We assumed that's why Mrs Hexham's last words were "you traitor". She was talking to Madame Dubois.'

'That was something of a "wild goose chase", said Shaw. 'After I re-visited the village hall and thought about Mrs Hexham's position on the floor when she died, I realised that once the curtain had fallen down she would not only have had Madame Dubois in her line of sight, but Mr

Hexham also.'

'It was her husband who was the "traitor"', said McPherson.

'Quite possibly,' said Shaw. 'We shall never know. But the more interesting revelations from the newspaper library concerned the Hexhams, not Madame Dubois. Mr Hexham's business was in financial difficulties, and Mrs Hexham had recently come into a large sum of money following her father's death.'

'I see,' said Gutteridge. 'They said in the court report it had something to do with an inheritance. Makes sense. Hexham bumped off his wife to get her money. But wouldn't he have got it anyway?'

'No,' said Ludd. 'That came out in court. Mrs Hexham's father's will put the money in a trust that was only to be used by her.'

'Her old man didn't trust the husband, then?' asked Gutteridge.

'Possibly,' said Ludd. 'But he didn't mistrust him enough to think Hexham would kill his wife to get the money, because there was nothing in the will saying he wouldn't get it in the event of Mrs Hexham's untimely death.'

'That would require a degree of suspicion highly uncommon in most people,' mused Shaw.

'Oh, and that Madame Dubois is a Roman, isn't she?' asked Gutteridge. 'They all are, the Belgians.'

'What about it?' asked Ludd. 'Stick to the point, won't you?'

'I am, chief,' said Gutteridge. 'Roman Catholics don't allow divorce, do they? So Madame couldn't hope to set up a happy home with Hexham, even if he divorced his wife. She'd be, what do you call it, ex-disconnected. Right, vicar?'

'Excommunicated,' said Shaw. 'That did occur to me also as a reason why Hexham might kill his wife, in addition to wanting her money.'

'That's pretty much what Hexham admitted to,' said Ludd. He shook his head. 'What kind of a world do we live in when someone kills his wife not just for her money but because his fancy woman and co-conspirator wants to keep in with her church.'

'The desire for "respectability" can lead to all sorts of sinfulness, Chief Inspector,' said Shaw. 'Remember that Madame Dubois had already had to face social ostracisation in her native Belgium. She presumably did not wish for the reputation she had built here in England to be ruined also by a divorce scandal. There was also her son to think of. '

'I suppose so,' said Ludd. 'Must take a rum sort of chap to murder his own wife though. Mrs Ludd can be trying at times and I daresay I am to her, but I mean, neither of us would kill the other.'

'Sadly the Hexhams did not seem to have a happy marriage,' said Shaw. 'I saw for myself how she spoke to him in public, and I dread to think what it was like in private.'

'I suppose so,' said Ludd. 'This fits in more or less with what Hexham and Madame Dubois told us when we interviewed them. His wife treated him like dirt, he said. Madame Dubois was kind to him, and he was flattering to her, a lonely widow, and well, one thing led to the other and before long they *both* wanted rid of Mrs Hexham. Sang like canaries they did – so much for the great romance, they accused each other of everything, and that's how I got 'em convicted.'

'Hang on a minute, vicar,' said Gutteridge. 'How does all this fit in with Weekes? Why did *he* stab Mrs Hexham?

Did Hexham pay him, or something?'

'I was suspicious,' said Shaw,' of *both* Hexham and Weekes after I erected a substitute curtain in the village hall, and realised that the assertion that Hexham and Weekes both made, that it was too dark to see anything behind the curtain, was patently false.'

'We worked out it must have been one of those two, at about the same time, but for a different reason,' said Ludd proudly. 'The medical report from the doctor showed Mrs Hexham had been stabbed twice, so we knew it had to be someone behind that curtain that did it, because everyone saw Havering stab her just once.'

'How on earth didn't you notice she'd been stabbed twice before?' asked Gutteridge incredulously. 'Didn't you check the body?'

'Of course we did,' growled McPherson. 'But the stab wounds were both in the same place with a similar knife. Hexham must have realised he had to take care to stab in the same place, and he managed it – it took a careful medical examination to work that out.'

'All right Jock, all right,' said Gutteridge. 'I was only asking.'

'And it's Detective Sergeant McPherson to you, not "Jock",' warned the Scotsman.

'If I might continue…' interjected Shaw, politely but firmly. 'I suspected Weekes as being the more likely of the two men to have murdered Mrs Hexham, because, although he claimed not to have received a blackmail letter, Havering claimed to have seen him reading something which looked very similar to the letter that *he* received. And, if it it was Mrs Hexham's plan to blackmail *all* the members of the committee into allowing her to remain in the group, it seemed highly likely that he would have received a letter also. That is why I visited him first, thinking him the more likely suspect.'

'We came to the same conclusions,' said Ludd. 'I placed constables on watch to make sure neither Weekes nor Hexham could make a run for it, and we came as quick as we could. But Weekes had already tried to hang himself, and left a full confession, so that was that.'

'Until the vicar had other ideas, eh?' said Gutteridge.

'I must admit,' said Shaw, 'that I had no definite evidence against Madame Dubois and Hexham. It was only circumstantial, whereas Weekes had written a full confession. But there was one more odd detail that made me uneasy.'

'Which was?' asked Gutteridge.

Shaw took another sip of beer. 'Excellent mild,' he murmured. 'On the way towards Mr Weekes' cottage I chanced to see Albert Cranston walking in the other direction, carrying what looked like a rifle or shotgun. It occurred to me that perhaps somebody had forced Weekes at gunpoint to write his confession, and then hang himself. Otherwise it all seemed too convenient.'

'Why on earth would someone do that?' asked Gutteridge. 'I'd have a go at the blighter, at least I'd have a chance.'

'Perhaps,' said Shaw. 'But perhaps Weekes thought he might have a chance if he went along with it – that he might be able to get out of it at the last minute somehow, but never managed it. Perhaps…he even wanted to die. I suspect Mr Weekes is a deeply unhappy man.'

'But what was Cranston's motive?' asked Gutteridge 'Why wasn't he pinched by the coppers as well?'

'Mr Cranston is entirely innocent,' said Shaw. 'I soon found out,' he continued, 'that he had not come from Weekes' cottage – but that he had been to Mr Hexham's house to collect his rifle, which Mr Hexham borrowed on the pretext of shooting rats in his corn store.'

'When he was really using it to force Weekes at gunpoint to write a confession then kill himself,' said Gutteridge.

'Yes,' replied Shaw. 'Hexham had forced Mr Weekes to sign a confession at gunpoint, and then hang himself. Unfortunately the poor man was not brave enough to call Hexham's bluff and force him to shoot, as that would have upset the entire scheme. He perhaps did think he could somehow release himself from the noose before it was too late, but was unable to.

'Mr Weekes, it seems, had already been threatened behind the curtain by Mr Hexham, who after he had stabbed his wife, told poor Mr Weekes that the same would happen to him if he told anyone the truth. He was too frightened to go to the police.'

'From what we were able to work out,' said Ludd, 'Hexham was working on the assumption that the knife thrust through the curtain from Havering would be enough to kill his wife. But it wasn't – the doctor said that blow was only a small flesh wound.

'Hexham realised and put his back-up plan into operation – to stab his wife again using a similar knife in the same place to make sure she was dead, but with it hopefully appearing as if she had only been stabbed *once*. It was a long shot, but he had to make sure she didn't live to tell the tale. He told me he knew he could manage it without being seen by Weekes because it would be dark behind the curtain. '

'But how,' asked Gutteridge, 'could he be sure he'd stab her in the right place if it was going to be so dark that Weekes couldn't see him?'

'Told me he was going to feel for the cut on her clothing from Havering's stab, and use that as a guide,' said Ludd.

Gutteridge shivered. 'Grisly, isn't it?'

'I've known worse things,' said Ludd with a shrug. 'Hexham seemed quite proud of the idea, like he'd worked out some theatrical special effect.'

'In the end, he was able to see exactly what he was doing,' said Shaw, 'because a *different* curtain had to be used. The original one, used in rehearsals, had disintegrated and was being mended. The substitute curtain was thinner – I distinctly recall Mrs Hexham saying it looked like a dust-sheet – and enabled enough light to penetrate it for Mr Hexham to see to stab his wife in exactly the right place. The problem was, of course, that it was then also possible for Mr Weekes to witness it.'

'I still don't see why Hexham had to bump off Weekes if everyone thought Havering was the killer,' said Gutteridge.

'Despite threatening Mr Weekes to prevent him going to the police,' said Shaw, 'Mr Hexham knew he could not trust him, and the best thing to do was to murder him also. Once it became known that the murder charges against Mr Havering – the original scapegoat – had been dropped, he formed the plan to force Mr Weekes to confess and then falsify his suicide.'

'Yes,' said Ludd. 'Hexham never fully confessed to that but Madame Dubois gave us the full details. We played them off against each other nicely.'

'Wait a minute,' said Gutteridge, after he knocked back the contents of his second whisky glass, 'if it was Hexham that stabbed his wife, why all this palava with Havering and the dummy knife?'

'From what the Chief Inspector tells me following his questioning of Mr Hexham and Madame Dubois,' said Shaw, 'the substitution of the dummy dagger was an elaborate ruse to deflect suspicion on to Havering, to either make it look like a terrible accident, or an actual murder. It did not particularly matter which.'

'Hang on half a mo,' said Gutteridge. 'Tell me more about this dagger substitution. I don't follow.'

'Havering claimed,' said Shaw, 'that he took what he thought was the dummy knife from the properties cupboard, and he only realised it was a real knife when he stabbed Mrs Hexham through the curtain.'

'Yes, he was sick as a dog after he told us that,' said Ludd. 'Did make me wonder for a moment if he was telling the truth about not knowing the knife was real.'

'Didn't stop you charging him though, did it?' said Gutteridge.

'Now look here...' began Ludd.

'*If* I might continue,' said Shaw.

'Go on,' said Ludd, folding his arms.

'Thank you, Chief Inspector,' replied the cleric. 'It was possible, of course, that Havering was lying and that he knew all along he had the real knife and that saying he thought he had the dummy one was just a clever ruse to make the murder of Mrs Hexham appear to be an accident.

'But after it became apparent that someone *behind* the curtain also stabbed Mrs Hexham, and that it was the fatal blow that was administered by that someone, it seemed likely that Havering was telling the truth; he really *did* take the dummy knife from the properties cupboard and really did believe he was using it to stab "Polonius" through the curtain.'

'Wait a minute,' said Gutteridge, looking up from his notebook and taking a long draught of beer. 'If Havering took the dummy knife on stage, how did he stab Mrs Hexham with it? You've all said there were two stab wounds, I thought?'

'The dummy knife was substituted deftly by somebody

on stage,' replied Shaw. 'Havering, in the character of Hamlet, had the dagger in a scabbard on his belt. When his mother – Madame Dubois, that is – embraced him, she took the opportunity to switch the dummy knife for a real one, which looked very similar. In the brief moment that he took out the dagger and stabbed it through the curtain, he did not realise a substitution had occurred. Why would he?'

Gutteridge whistled. 'Lord, that was a clever trick.'

'It was,' said Ludd. 'She told us she had the dagger concealed in her frock and all she had to do was switch it over with the one in Havering's belt when they embraced. She practiced it with Hexham at his house until they got it right.'

'But hang on,' said Gutteridge. 'How come Madame Dubois' dabs didn't appear on the knife?'

'Dabs?' asked Shaw.

'He means fingerprints,' said McPherson. 'There weren't any, because that Madame Dubois was wearing gloves as part of her costume.'

'As any royal Shakespearian character would have done,' said Shaw. 'I only became suspicious that that might have been how it was done, because I recalled that Madame Dubois was so insistent on putting the embrace into the scene, when it does not appear in the stage directions. And because it was Madame Dubois who "found" the dummy dagger by the side of the stage.'

'And you assumed Havering had just left it there when he switched the dummy dagger for the real one, before he went on stage?' asked Gutteridge.

'Something like that,' said Shaw. 'But I never particularly suspected Havering. It seemed fantastical that he would carry out such a daring attack in full view of at least fifty people.'

'Hexham's plan was pretty fantastical as well though,' said Gutteridge. 'It could all have easily backfired.'

'Yes, but he was desperate,' said Ludd. 'He needed that money and his wife had driven him half-barmy with her nagging over the years. He didn't even bother making the working knife look completely like the dummy one. He just painted the jewels on because, he said, Cranston's store had run out of them and he hadn't time to find any more.'

'That did, however, work in his favour,' said Shaw.

'How so?' asked Gutteridge.

'Because if the real knife did not look exactly like the dummy knife,' explained Shaw, 'it would make a jury even less likely to think that Mr Havering picked up the wrong weapon by accident.'

'But all this is theories, vicar,' said Gutteridge. 'You said yourself you weren't certain enough about anything to bother the Chief, I mean, the Chief Inspector here about it.'

'Quite so,' said Shaw. 'I knew I needed definite proof that Madame Dubois and Mr Hexham were involved. That is why I gave you the "tip off" about Mr Weekes' confession on the telephone. Chief Inspector Ludd was rather angry about it, but it was necessary.'

'Why?' enquired Gutteridge.

'I needed to do something to draw out Madame Dubois and Mr Hexham into incriminating themselves. It occurred to me that if it were generally known that Mr Weekes might be about to make a recovery, that Mr Hexham might attempt to finish the job he began in the cottage.'

'I still don't see why you couldn't just have invited them to visit him in hospital,' said Ludd, 'instead of blabbing to the papers.'

'They might have suspected something had I done that,' said Shaw. 'It was better that the information reach them from the newspapers rather than directly from me. That was why, Mr Gutteridge, I expressed a certain amount of righteous anger on the telephone to you when I discovered you had linked the article on Mr Weekes' confession with my name.'

'Cor,' said Gutteridge to Ludd and McPherson. 'You should have heard him! Now it makes sense. Well, I hope that apology I printed the next day was enough for you.'

'Indeed it was,' said Shaw, 'or you and I would not be conversing today. Suffice to say, the ruse worked. I visited Madame Dubois and alluded – truthfully, I might add – to the fact that Mr Weekes had mentioned her name, and that he seemed about to make a recovery, but that his life hung in the balance. I hinted that the police guard might be lifted in order for her to have a few private moments with him, and the trap was set.'

'It was rather irregular, I must admit,' said Ludd, 'but I agreed with Mr Shaw that it was worth a try in order to test his theory about Hexham and Madame Dubois. If it didn't work, there would be no harm done – I made sure of that from the doctor who said Weekes was definitely getting better so I knew he'd soon be talking to us.

'Sergeant McPherson and myself secreted ourselves in the bathroom and waited; sure enough, once Madame Dubois thought she was alone, she took a pillow and started to smother Weekes with it. Fortunately the man was sedated, and didn't notice a thing.

'Mr Shaw saw a man outside the room and PC Arbon apprehended him. It was Hexham, who was lurking by the French doors. Seems Madame Dubois wasn't sure if she could go through with it herself and he was waiting there to give her a hand if her nerve went. The plan was, apparently, to suffocate him and then for Madame to shout for help and say Weekes was unresponsive. Once he was dead they hoped we would believe he just slipped away.'

'Suffocation is, I believe, very difficult to prove,' said Shaw.

'Correct,' said Ludd. 'Especially with a patient who was already weakened and with a damaged respiratory system. They could well have got away with it if we hadn't been waiting for them. Once they knew the game was up, they started denouncing each other and it was child's play to make the charges stick.'

'That is about all there is to say,' said Shaw. 'Other than that I am pleased to see that Mr Weekes has made an almost complete recovery. He is planning to retire quietly to Le Touquet, where he will be able to visit his mother in Eastbourne quite easily on the cross channel steamer.'

'Oh ho!' said Gutteridge. 'No law against his sort over there, I suppose? Well, you know what the French are like...'

'It is none of our business,' said Shaw firmly. 'We can hardly blame him for wishing to move abroad, and thus should simply give thanks for his recovery from such a dreadful ordeal.'

'Well I'd best dash,' said Gutteridge, closing his notebook and knocking back the remainders of beer and whisky that were in the glasses in front of him. 'If I get started now I'll make tomorrow's edition.'

'And mind you tell the whole truth and nothing but the truth,' warned Ludd. 'I don't want to see any made up nonsense in your article.'

'Now look here,' said Gutteridge. 'Would I do a thing like that?'

'Yes,' said McPherson gruffly.

'Now *you* look here,' said Ludd, pointing an official looking finger at the reporter. 'I've got my eye on you and if I find you've printed anything derogatory about us, or any fancy stories about Mr Shaw, who's a respectable clergyman, you'll be for it.'

'This isn't Soviet Russia,' said Gutteridge, somewhat doubtfully. 'The police can't just tell the press what to do.'

'No and nor should they,' said Ludd, 'if the press do their job properly. But you've already written a lot of nonsense about Mr Shaw...'

'For which I apologised...' said Gutteridge.

'For which you apologised,' echoed Ludd, 'but don't you do that again, because if you do...'

'You'll what?' asked Gutteridge.

'You've had four pints of strong beer and four large whiskies while we've been talking,' said Ludd.

'And?' said Gutteridge. 'That's just my afternoon tea, that is.'

'I thought so,' said Ludd. 'And that's your Austin Seven outside, isn't it? Registration BJ 164.'

'You ought to know,' replied Gutteridge. 'It was you that threatened to tip it over with me in it last time we met. What about it?'

'You write a nice little article with no funny business my lad,' warned Ludd, 'or I'll tell every bobby from here to Norwich to stop your car if ever they see it. Because if they do they'll most likely find you're drunk in charge of a motor vehicle, which as I am sure you know is an offence under the Road Traffic Act 1930.'

'Well...I....' stammered Gutteridge.

'And if you *are* drunk,' continued Ludd, 'I'll put in a word to make sure the magistrate takes away your driving licence. I don't think you'll be catching many "exclusives" if you have to go around on a bicycle, do you?'

'All right, all right,' said Gutteridge. 'I'll make sure the article's the Gospel truth – no offence, vicar. I'll even read a copy of it over the telephone to you before I dictate it to the news desk. How's that?'

'That will not be necessary,' said Shaw, as he reached for his panama hat. 'Where would we be if we did not trust one another?'

Shaw's offering of an 'exclusive' was not solely due to his gratitude for Gutteridge's research in the newspaper library. It also made it much easier for Shaw – or rather, Hettie – to get rid of any other journalists who called at the vicarage asking for interviews. Once the court case had ended, the gentlemen of the press had lost interest, and peace and silence returned to the village of Lower Addenham.

'I'm so glad that reporter wrote a nice article about you,' said Mrs Shaw as she poured afternoon tea while they sat in the sitting room. She gestured to the two-day-old newspaper which sat on the tea-table next to her.

'And even a photograph of you and the detectives. A good one, too.'

'Yes, it was refreshing to read a straightforward report, without sensationalism,' mused Shaw as he took a sip of tea from his cup. 'Unfortunately, Mr Havering and Miss Kersey were not treated so well by Mr Gutteridge in his article about *them*.'

'Which article?' asked Mrs Shaw.

'In today's *Chronicle*,' replied her husband.

'Has the case ended?'

Shaw cleared his throat. He felt rather uncomfortable discussing the matter with his wife, but he knew she was something of a 'woman of the world,' having spent some time in her younger days volunteering at a church home for unmarried mothers.

'Indeed it has. The doctor in the case has been jailed for two years. Havering received a sentence of six months.'

'And Miss Kersey?'

'Eighteen months. I shall visit her of course.'

'But that's appalling,' said Mrs Shaw. 'From what you told me, she never would have gone through with it if Havering hadn't bullied her into it and paid for it.'

'The judge stated that ultimately it was her responsibility,' said Shaw.

Mrs Shaw frowned, and clattered her tea cup against its saucer.

'The judge obviously hasn't an iota of understanding of what men such as Ronald Havering are like and the way they manipulate young women. Not to mention the doctors who profit from it. Oh Lucian, if only she had come to you first.'

'You are quite right, my dear,' said Shaw. 'I should take more interest in our young people and their problems. It is an uncertain world in which they have come of age, unlike our time before the war. Things seemed simpler then.'

'Before you become too nostalgic,' said Mrs Shaw, 'how do you propose to take more interest in the young people of the parish?'

'By encouraging wholesome social activity,' said Shaw. 'An alternative to the public houses and the dance-halls where the likes of Havering seek their prey.'

'Do go on.'

'I visited young Mrs Cranston today at the Stores,' said Shaw. 'She wishes to start a new amateur theatrical company to replace the now defunct Lower Addenham Dramatic Society. It will be called the Addenham Players, and will be aimed at the younger generation. She has asked for the group to have strong links with the church, so I have asked Laithwaite to supervise it, and he has agreed.'

'Your poor overworked curate,' said Mrs Shaw. 'Why couldn't *you* run the group?'

'My dear, I am far too much of an Edwardian relic to be actively involved in youth work. Except, of course, youth work for the very young, which I will soon be offering to Mr and Mrs Cranston.'

'What on earth do you mean?'

'Baptism, of course. She told me this morning that she is expecting.'

'Oh Lucian, that *is* good news. But I thought the doctors said…'

'Doctors can be wrong,' said Shaw. 'Sometimes very wrong'.

He looked at his watch. 'In fact, that reminds me. I said that Mrs Cranston and I ought to recite the Magnificat in church, and she agreed.'

A few minutes later Shaw and the youthful Mrs Cranston, with a mysterious new bloom in her features, knelt in the ancient parish church, and the words of the Song of Mary drifted out through the open door into the late summer haze.

'For He that is mighty hath magnified me, and holy is His name…'

Other books by **Hugh Morrison**

A Third Class Murder (Reverend Shaw's first case)
An antiques dealer is found robbed and murdered in a third class train compartment on a remote Suffolk branch line. The Reverend Lucian Shaw, who was travelling on the same train, is concerned that the police have arrested the wrong man, and begins an investigation of his own.

The King is Dead
An exiled Balkan king is shot dead in his secluded mansion following a meeting with the local vicar, Reverend Lucian Shaw. Shaw believes that the culprit is closer than the police think, and before long is on the trail of a desperate killer who will stop at nothing to evade capture.

The Wooden Witness
After finding the battered corpse of a spiritualist medium at an archaeological site on the Suffolk coast, the Reverend Lucian Shaw is thrust into a dark and deadly mystery involving ancient texts and modern technology.

Death on the Night Train
Reverend Shaw is called to the deathbed of an elderly relative in Scotland by an anonymous telegram. Soon he becomes embroiled in a fiendish conspiracy which reaches to the highest levels of the British establishment.

Published by Montpelier Publishing
Available from Amazon or your local bookshop

Printed in Great Britain
by Amazon